STOLEN BY THE SHADOWS

INTERNATIONAL BESTSELLING AUTHOR

SARAH SPADE

Cover by Fran of Merry-Book-Round

Interior Art by Claire of Luminescence Covers

FOREWORD

Thank you for checking out *Stolen by the Shadows*!

This is the second book in the **Sombra Demons** series, though chronologically it's set before *Mated to the Monster*. It tells the story of Amy and Nox, the bonded couple that Shannon and Mal visit in Connecticut. Like the first book, it's a standalone, and it is written for readers 18+ for the steamy scenes and potentially triggering content.

In this book, Amy is hiding out from an ex-boyfriend who doesn't understand that the word 'no' is a complete sentence. There's no SA on page, but there is reference to Connor trying to push her to go farther with him than she was comfortable with before she left him. Then he stalks her and chases her, his obsession getting in the way of Amy's HEA with Nox. Because this is a Sarah Spade book, he gets what's coming to him when Nox finally gets his claws on him, but I want readers to understand Amy has a good reason for being in need of her protector when the book begins.

This book will also touch on the fact that Nox met Amy when she was a child. I want to make it clear here: at no point did he think of her sexually while she was young. He recognized that she would be his mate when she was grown up and a mature female, and their mate bond doesn't fully trigger until they meet again when she's twenty-six. I know there's the power dynamic that comes with him being someone she knew from a young age, but he's also a 1200-year-old shadow demon from another realm falling head over heels for a twenty-six-year-old human chick he'd sacrifice his freedom and his life for so, really, Amy kinda has most of the power during their mating.

Oh, and just a quick reminder: this takes place about fifteen years before Shannon and Mal's story. Though I usually don't give my books a firm time period so that it doesn't throw readers off in the years to come, I made an exception with this book. *Stolen by the Shadows* is set in 2007, and I had a lot of fun throwing nods to that time period in with this story!

Also, like the first book, insta-love is a thing, protective hunters are sexy in a different way than sweet himbo demons, fated mate bonds can never be wrong in this universe, and there's no need for protection because a) demons don't get diseases, b) Nox and Amy are both virgins, and c) she can only get pregnant during the night of the gold moon, and they don't plan on having offspring for a very long time. But they will have a HEA, and I hope you enjoy coming along for the ride with these two :)

xoxo,

Sarah

PROLOGUE

NOX

The legends are real.

For all of my centuries, I've heard stories of a mortal race living in a realm far from Sombra where my people reside. Weak creatures with no horns, claws, or fangs to protect them. A lifespan that's over in the blink of an eye. Rounded ears. Pale skin. A monster so utterly different from demonkind that it was a relief when Duke Haures refused to allow any of his subjects to cross planes into the human world.

That was two thousand years ago when he became ruler of Sombra and enacted his laws, long before I even existed. I've twelve centuries now, more or less, so I always knew of the warnings, the whispers, and the duke's tenets. But I'm also a male.

A Sombra male who'd hoped and hunted and secretly wished for a female companion of my own. A *mate*. And when centuries passed and none called to me, either in my clan or on my land, or even any of our neighboring planes… I started to grow curious about the race of creatures spoken of as legend.

Humans are considered forbidden fruit for obvious reasons. The duke's first law is that none of our kind is allowed to cross into the mortal plane. There's just one exception, and that's when a portal opens and magic summons us to the other world; that only happens when a Sombra demon's one true mate is a human capable of manifesting us to their realm with their unique magics.

When the spell lashed me during a hunt, there was enough time for me to drop my bow and arrow before I was yanked through the portal and dropped in a den of dark shadows, immediately free to prowl around the space, searching for the human female who called me to her. I could… I could *scent* her. Like sweets and the rare breeze in dry, arid Sombra, she was near, though I didn't see her.

No worries. I would find her. The one female meant for me and me alone… I'd find her, I'd claim her, and I would finally have someone to provide for that wasn't just part of the clan. A soul who would love me as her own, and not fear my reputation as a dangerous male, more demonic than most other

Sombrans. She'd be mine, as I'd be hers, and nothing would separate us as long as I drew breath.

I'd waited for twelve centuries. With her sweet scent in my lungs, I'm not sure I could wait a second longer—until I hear the smallest of gasps, followed by the pounding beat of a frightened heart.

I appeared in my shadow form, golden runes from the magic traveling down my black arms. Throwing back my head, I was prepared to show off my horns, my build, my body, hoping that my mate would be pleased by what she saw.

Once the stink of fear seeped into her scent, over-powering the sweet, I slunk further into the shadows in the corner of the room.

I wait. Always, I wait.

And that's when she slithers out from beneath the stack of bedding across from me, I see her for the first time, and I accept that I waited twelve hundred and sixty-three years… and I'm not done waiting for my mate just yet.

My beloved mate who, rising up to her knees, voice full of both terror and youthful wonder, asks me in the human tongue that I don't yet understand: "Are you the bogeyman?"

I AM NOX.

I am a hunter. The most powerful one in all of

Nuit. I provide the meat for my clan, and also protect my fellow demons from the dangers that lurk along the edge of our settlement's shadows. No one is stronger than I am in the clan, or more fierce. Why shouldn't I be given a delicate human as a mate? She'll need protection, and no one shall be a better guardian and protector than I.

Only… she's spawn. A *child*. Not even a decade old in her time, that's the same as a Sombra demon reaching their first century. My kind aren't fully mature until our third, and while I won't have to wait so long to give my essence to Amelia and take her as my bonded mate, I have at least another decade in human years before then.

I know that I should stay away. If the duke discovered that I was returning to the human world whenever I had the chance, I'd be in chains before I knew it. I'm exploiting a loophole so rare, I don't think it even occurred to the ruler of Sombra to be possible. We are only allowed to cross over when our mate summons us. Once a mate bond is triggered, we have until the next gold moon to finalize it before we either release our mates or end up in the duke's dungeons.

But I don't have a bond with Amelia. Not a true mate bond, at least. What we have is a whisper, the promise of forever once she's old enough to understand that, as she's meant for me, I am meant for her. For now, I'm her companion. Her… friend.

Her shadow man.

My mate, on the other claw, is inquisitive. Sharp. Absolutely delightful.

Without a bond, there is no essence exchange. I only know her name because she tapped her chest and repeated it, showing no fear despite the way it once lingered in her scent. I told her I was Nox, but anytime I visit Amelia, I purposely stay in my shadow form. She's not afraid of the dark, billowy figure with the glowing red gaze, but compared to her pale skin, her rich shadow-dark hair and matching eyes, I'm not so sure my true demon form wouldn't terrify her.

Besides, I won't deny I'm skirting the edge of the duke's first law. For any Sombra demons who find a path to the human world, we are not allowed to be seen. So long as I only visit Amelia at night, hiding in the shadows, I can plead ignorance.

Not my tiny female. And though the mate's promise will have to wait until she's older, I gave her my solemn vow the night she summoned me while searching for another: I will do whatever I must to keep her safe.

Thank the gods, she believes me. Better yet, she *trusts* me.

As she should.

It isn't long before the fear fades entirely, and she is notably pleased when I come to see her during the time of shadows in the human realm. She's also looking for answers that I do not have. First, it's because we can not communicate. Without my essence, she doesn't understand the Sombran tongue just as I do not know her human language; once I have her essence, I will, though not until then. But she's determined. And smart. Over the next year, she insists on learning enough Sombran that we can actually talk. In no time, she's fluent, and I have to work hard not to admit to her that her fate is forever tied to mine once she knows what I'm saying.

She'd hear me, but she wouldn't understand—and it's essential that she must.

So, again, I wait.

A bogeyman, I discover, is a type of monster. So, it seems, is a Sombra demon. My Amy—her name is Amelia, but she tells me she's Amy—is convinced I'm a nice monster. I'm not her kin, like she hoped I'd be when she read the words that summoned me to her quarters, but I make her feel safe. With her mother sad and her father gone, she likes feeling safe.

And I… I like learning every detail about my future mate that I can.

Once her spell summoned me to her world, there's a path between my home and hers. It takes but a drop of essence to visit her. So long as I don't touch her, don't mark her in any way, hopefully the duke won't notice that I spend as much time in the human realm as I do.

I still tend to my clan. I hunt with a fervor that frightens some of my clansmen. A worthy male must prove himself, and I trade meat with the builders to turn my small hut into a home fit for my mate. I also make sure that the true monsters and carnivores that lurk along the edge of Sombra's shadows know better than to target Nuit. Even with my Amy still in her human world, I must make it so that she's protected anywhere and, eventually, she will join me in Sombra.

I'll insist on it.

Time passes. She grows older under my watchful gaze. Still not ready to be my mate—or for her to even understand the truth behind my continued visits to her world—but her delicate little chin lifts when I chuckle and tell her that, to me, she's still spawn. She retorts that she's twelve with a fierceness that echoes my protective instinct toward her.

It's been three human years since her spell called me to her. Before Amy, that length of time would've seemed like a blink of an eye to such a long-lived creature as I. Now? Every day without her seems an eternity, but I am determined. I will keep her my secret while preparing for the life we'll have one day, just as I'll risk being caught by Duke Haures and his soldiers with every trip through the portal I take.

I'm a fool, though. So caught up in the promise of claiming my mate, I'm reckless.

I let her touch me.

It was innocent. A simple brush of her pale fingers

when, for the countless time, she marveled at what my shadowed form would feel like against her skin. I'd always refused her, knowing that was a dangerous game to play with my Amy, but already I knew I could deny her nothing when she pleaded with me the way she had. She touched me, and though the mate bond stayed dormant and we didn't exchange essence, it was enough.

The duke found out. Of course he did. He found out, and the next time I visit Amy, the portal opens behind me to reveal three other demons in their shadows: Glaine and Sammael, two of Duke Haures's top soldiers, and Apollyon, my clan leader.

I know then that I've been found out, but nothing will stop me from protecting my mate.

Thank the gods that she was quick to react. As soon as the shadows in her bedroom began to gather, a sign that a portal was about to open, I barked at her to hide and she listened. Just like the first night she called me to her, she slipped under her bedding, out of sight.

Another Sombra demon would be able to sniff her out if they got the chance, but as I pull myself up to my full height, hovering off of the floor as rage fuels me, I refuse to let them try.

Apollyon hangs back. So does Sammael. Glaine, with his glowing green eyes, takes the lead.

"You know why we've come, Nox. You've tested Duke Haures's patience for the last time. He allowed you to cross into this realm because your fated mate was part of it, but still you return and you have not bonded her to you."

I could not. Glaine—and the duke—must understand.

"She's not mature enough to be a mate. I protect her. That's all I've been doing."

"You touched her." His eyes brighten even as the golden runes fade against his inky black form. "You marked her."

"I did not—"

"You did," interjects Sammael. He's the duke's mage. A conjurer as much as a soldier, if he's here with Glaine, then I know that my fate's already sealed. "You're aware that Duke Haures senses whenever a portal off-plane is open."

It's not a question. "I am."

"Then you're also aware that he's been informed of your every trip to watch over your mate. Mature or not, you know the laws. By allowing her to touch you, she's taken some of your essence. She knows more about Sombra than any human is allowed. You must mate her or come with us."

Come with us… I know what that means.

I broke the duke's first law. There's only one punishment for that.

The cursed chains and a long stay in his dungeon.

"What about my human?" I demand.

"The duke will not punish the innocent," vows

Sammael. "So long as she speaks nothing of Sombra, you will be nothing more than a dream to her. I will ensure that myself."

"And me?"

"You broke the law, Nox," Apollyon says. My clan leader is apologetic. A good male, and one who would support me if he could—but he is not wrong. I knew what I was doing every time I left Sombra for my Amy's human world.

Just like I knew what exactly I'd done when I passed the tiniest bit of myself into her. I'd marked her as mine, though I couldn't have her—and now I most likely never will.

I hold out my wrists, prepared for the heavy weight of the manacles that will be clamped there. I only hope that they'll drag me through the portal before Amy gets her first peek at me in my true, demonic shape. I'm sure—from the worry coloring her scent, and the fear I'd hoped to never smell again—that I've already done enough damage tonight.

No more.

Jutting out my chin, I snarl, "Give me the chains."

For my mate, I take them gladly.

CHAPTER 1
HALLOWEEN CANDY

AMY

I freaking love Halloween.

It's always been my favorite holiday. Ever since I was a little kid, I looked forward to the chill in the air, the spooky movies, the visits to the pumpkin patches. Wearing matching costumes with my mom and Aunt Su; even before the divorce, my dad was too busy to tag along on family-friendly activities. Corn mazes… I had so much fun getting lost in corn mazes. And though I'm not much of an artist, I find it relaxing to trace the stencil on a pumpkin and carve the hell out of it.

My new apartment has six in various stages of decay. Back in Connecticut, everyone in our apartment complex got together to have a pumpkin carving contest in the days leading up to Halloween. We had a row of pumpkins lined up every year, and never had to worry about anyone in Madison smashing them.

I don't know my new neighbors well enough to leave them outside. I did put one out in the hall after I carved it last week, but a freckled redheaded boy knocked on my door with an impish smile, a stuttered apology, and my squished pumpkin. Apparently he'd run down the hall, tripped and fallen on it.

Since then, I've decorated my apartment with them. I still have another night before it's Halloween—today's the 29th of October—and I'm just a tiny bit worried about drawing attention to myself when it's Mischief Night. I mean, a little TPing never hurt anyone, and I got egged once when I was in middle school, but I don't want to leave a pumpkin out for someone to grab and get into trouble with tomorrow night.

I knew what to expect in Madison during the holiday season. Only… I'm not in Madison anymore. Since the third week of July, I've been a Jersey girl. When I had to get out of Connecticut and fast, my old college roomie, Laura, told me about an apartment in Jersey City that I could afford to sublet while still working to get my new business off the ground.

I went to Wesleyan University for four years. I got my BA in history with a minor in sociology; whenever my mom pointed out that Laura was kinda the only friend I made during my four years (and only because she shared a dorm room with me), I reminded her what I learned about humans in the past and how they thought definitely backed up my long-held position of being a content loner. Of course, after I graduated in 2003 and moved back in with Mom, I couldn't figure out a way to make my degree work for me—so I took some business classes.

I had this grand idea of setting up a home business where I was my own boss. All the English courses I took as an undergrad, plus a love of reading, made me think about going into freelance editing or something like that. To make sure I could run the business side of it, I enrolled for the spring at the beginning of last year. Classes started in January, and that's when I first met Connor Hart…

Ugh. Just thinking his name has my stomach going tight. Three months since I snuck out in the night so that my ex wouldn't know where I was going, and I still haven't been able to shake the suspicion that he's simply biding his time, waiting for me to change my mind and go back to him.

Yeah, right. After what he did to me… after what he *could* have done if my mom hadn't had the best timing on the planet… I want nothing to do with Connor. I moved a state away to escape him, changing my number and altering my life plan so that I wouldn't be tied to him anymore. If I never see him again, that would be too soon.

At least I like my apartment. It has a cozy kitchen.

Since I'm currently subletting it from one of Laura's friends, it's pre-furnished which made hiding out as quick as I did even easier. A bathroom with a glass shower stall and decent water pressure. A bedroom that hasn't been tainted by a guy trying to drag my pants off of me while I tell him no—

A lump lodges in my throat. I swallow it roughly, pushing away from the table off of the kitchen where I was sitting, carving my seventh pumpkin. As the intrusive thought popped into my brain, my hand slipped. The cat I was carving nearly lost its tail when the knife moved so suddenly.

Toothpick. Don't think about Connor, Amy. Go find a toothpick or something to salvage the poor tail.

I scurry into my kitchen.

See? This is why I have six-and-a-half carved pumpkins in my living room. Whenever the past tries to worm its way into my brain, I need something to focus on that isn't my terror that Connor won't give up. Television only does so much to distract me, and after the hundreds—if not thousands—of phone calls and text messages I received from Connor after he realized I was gone, I jump whenever I hear any kind of ringtone.

I never answered him. I made the mistake of listening to the voicemails he left in the beginning before I got nauseous at the sound of his voice. Same thing with the messages. Ninety-nine percent of them came across as apologetic and pleading. He loved me. He was sorry. He admitted that he knew that I made it clear that I wouldn't sleep with him until I told him I was ready, and after waiting the entire year-and-a-half that he considered me his property, he thought I was. Now he sees I wasn't, and won't I give him another chance.

Uh-uh. No. Not gonna happen.

On the plus side, after I ditched my old phone, I didn't have to deal with that any longer. Once my mom threatened him with a restraining order if he didn't stop coming to her apartment to ask her to get in touch with me, he left her alone. Other than Laura, no one else knows where I am. Even my dad, who I haven't talked to since I graduated and he made sure I wouldn't need another check for the next semester, has no clue.

Good. Laura already swore she'd take the secret to her grave, and after Aunt Su disappeared when I was nine and my dad took off, it's been me and Mom against the world. I know she's got my back.

Actually, when I told her that I wanted to move out and confessed why, I had to remind her that she's a nurse. Nurses don't kill people, even if they try to sexually assault their daughter, and she does better work in the hospital than she would behind prison bars. She reluctantly agreed, then pushed me to tell the police.

I… I couldn't. Sure, I always knew my relationship with Connor was one-sided. He was into me way more than I was into him, but before I realized what kind of guy he was, I figured it didn't hurt to try. He was my first boyfriend and, if I'm being honest, I really only agreed to go out with him because he was super persistent, I was flattered because he's attractive, and my mom would joke that—despite being only twenty-five at the time—I was going to end up an old maid if I didn't start putting myself out there.

I think that's why she was so furious when Connor turned out to be as dangerous as he was. She feels guilty, thinking her comments pushed me into a relationship I didn't want. I tried to tell her it wasn't her fault, but all she did was offer to help me sneak away if that's what I wanted to do.

And I did. Leaving like a ghost in the night… it was the best thing for me. I get a little independence, I can still work on getting my business started since my mom refuses to let me pay my own rent until at least the new year, and I haven't heard from Connor in ages.

Plus, it's almost Halloween. Sure, it's the time of year you want to be scared, but I've enjoyed falling back into the nostalgia of my childhood. I've carved pumpkins I picked up from the farmer's market in downtown Jersey City, I put up some decorations that I bought from the dollar store a couple of blocks away from my apartment building, and I've watched every special that's come on the TV.

I haven't been this content in longer than I can remember. And if I'm lonely… well. That's nothing new. I grew up with an absentee dad, a workaholic mom who was overprotective when she was around, and the specter of Susanna Benoit, my mom's sister, hanging over my head.

She's been gone for most of my life. A research librarian who was a couple of years younger than my mom, she lived in Madison while my family was a couple of towns over. Up until I was eight, she was like a second mother figure to me. We even looked pretty similar, with the same dark brown hair and dark eyes. I spent so many weekends in her ranch-style home growing up, surrounded by her books and her infectious attitude. All these years later, the scent of a musty old library book makes me think of her. In her memory—and for my mom's sake after she took back her maiden name—I legally changed my name from Amelia Watterson to Amelia Benoit once I hit thirteen.

I was eight when she vanished. No one knows what happened to her. Her car was in the drive. Her house untouched. I overheard the police telling my mom that they think the Satanists had something to do with it—like, really?—because they found an old leather-bound book next to a chalk drawing on the floor, and a circle of salt.

I remember that book. It was written in Latin or

something. My aunt's life goal was to translate it, and when I heard that it was there and she wasn't, I knew something bad had happened to her. She went everywhere with that book.

That's why I took it. Before they locked up the house until she either came back or my mom decided what to do with it, I snuck into my aunt's house and stole her book. And then I—

Ah. Look at that. I've been rummaging around my kitchen, my thoughts rambling like a freight train in a bid to stop thinking about Connor for the umpteenth time. I almost forgot why I came in here in the first place. As soon as I see the tiny toothpick jar in the junk drawer, it comes rushing back.

I slip one out of its holder, then close the drawer. I'd bought the jar a couple of days ago when I made the same mistake with another of my pumpkins. Even though no one will see them but me, I like to do things the best I can.

I'm about to go back to the small table where I left my pumpkin when I hear a knock at my door. For a split second, I freeze. I have to remind myself that it can't be Connor. No way he found me on the sixth floor of a random apartment building in another state.

I toss the toothpick on the tabletop before heading to the front door. Because old habits die hard, I peek through the peephole. I see a flash of red hair and green eyes. Ah. Francesca Scott, the mother of Brendon, the freckled accidental pumpkin killer, and my neighbor from 6A.

She introduced herself to me after I'd been in my apartment for a month. She seems friendly enough, and since I can't think of a good reason to pretend she isn't out there, I unlock my door and pull it in.

She smiles. "Amy! I was hoping you were home."

I usually am. "Evening, Francesca. How are you?"

"Oh, I'm doing good. No complaints, right? You?"

As if I'd share my complaints with a stranger. Oh, no. I keep those to myself. "I'm great."

She peeks past my shoulder. "Looks like you're pretty ready for Halloween. I'm glad. That's actually why I stopped by. I was talking to Moira… you know Moira?"

I shake my head.

"She's 4D. The apartment, not the age, though she wouldn't mind claiming the age, either, I'll tell ya. Anyway, we realized that you're new to the building. Now, don't think I've been watching you or nothing, but I noticed you don't have any guy. No kids, either. We were worried you might not notice the holiday's coming up."

Thank you, Francesca. As if I didn't already know I lived alone. Now I have to deal with the paranoia that my neighbors are talking about that…

I give her a smile that I struggle to mean. On the

plus side, I'm being honest when I tell her, "I love Halloween."

"So you'll take part of trick-or-treating, won't you? Handing candies out to all the kids?"

Oh. "I… I guess." I hadn't been planning on it. A night where I had to face my fear every time the door-bell rang or someone knocked? I love Halloween, but I was hoping to leave my light off and pretend I wasn't home. "Do we get a bunch?"

"Tons," is Francesca's gleeful reply. "Every kid in the building knows to hit every door for their candy. Their friends come by, too. We turn it into a neigh-borhood affair."

We do? Oh, boy. "Okay. Thanks for letting me know. I'll have to make sure I get enough for Wednesday."

Her eyes go big. "You don't got any now?"

I've lived on the East Coast my whole life. I'm sure I have an accent. It's nothing compared to Francesca's Jersey accent. "Not yet, but I'll get some. Promise."

"Stores sell out, Amy. I don't even know if you'll be able to find any. You should go check."

"I will. First thing in the morning."

Francesca raises her eyebrows at me.

"Um. Okay. You know what? You're right." I don't like people all that much, but if there's one thing you can say about Amelia Benoit? She's too much of a people-pleaser for her own good. "Let me grab my hoodie and my purse."

I DROVE FROM CONNECTICUT TO NEW JERSEY. I HAVE a car. On the rare occasion I decide that I'm ready to face the world for a bit, I take it for a ride.

When I'm running down to the corner store for a Coke or even taking it a few blocks down for a pumpkin spice latte, I walk. To do a fast run for Halloween candy, I decide to get the exercise. It's not as chilly out as it can be, despite it being night, and a zip-up sweatshirt hoodie over my v-cut tee is enough for a quick trip out.

Francesca was right to kinda bully me into going now. The corner store? Fresh out of any kind of Halloween candy. All they had left was the king-sized bars, and that's too rich for my blood. Maybe if I only had a couple of kids to look forward to knocking on my door, I could. Since my neighbor makes it seem like I should be expecting a whole bunch, I need one of those huge mixed bags.

About three of four blocks down, I find a Quick Chek. Same thing. What I really need is to hit a Target or a Walmart, but that requires driving. It's late. Already dark. I don't want to head back to the underground parking where my car is at this hour only to have to go on a scavenger hunt for candy.

I get lucky when I hit my third store. A tiny, little no-name shop that I haven't seen yet since I moved to the area, the candy is overpriced, but at least it was a better bargain than buying fifty king-sized bars. I grab two huge mixed bags—one of candy, one of chocolates like Crunch bars and Butterfingers—and pay with my card. The plastic bag is heavy, but my hunt was successful. I will not disappoint my neighbor's kids this year.

Good job, Amy.

So pleased with myself, I forget to be as vigilant as I usually am when I'm out by myself. I think I got too complacent. All these months, Connor was just a bad memory. Out of sight, even if he wasn't out of my mind, I used to watch over my shoulder for him, just in case.

Wouldn't it figure that, one of the only times I don't, I catch a glimpse of him out of the corner of my eye.

Because that's him. Tall and slender, with a lean muscular build from his years of playing lacrosse, he's got on a black sweatshirt of his own and a pair of dark denim jeans as he lurks in the shadows. His sandy brown hair is short yet tousled in that casual look he has. Between that, his hazel eyes, and the single dimple that pops in his left cheek, he's the poster boy for the kind of guy you'd want to bring home to your mother.

I did, and she was as fooled as I was. Another reason she blames herself, but she isn't the only one. My gut told me that he was trouble. My brain told me to stay away.

My heart never even got involved… and my stomach goes queasy now as I realize he's here. Only a couple of blocks from where I am, as if he's been waiting near the street corner for me to come out and head back that way so I'd have to pass him, he's… he's *here*.

Connor. Here.

My fingers tighten around the handle of my plastic bag.

No. It can't be. I left him behind in Madison.

At least, I was supposed to have.

Then again, I learned my lesson the January before last. Obsession has nothing on Connor Hart. Once he decided I was his, he single-mindedly pursued me. I tried to refuse him gently. I tried to tell him I wasn't interested. I was in class to learn, not find a dude. He didn't care. He refused to give up, and… well. People-pleaser. I gave him a try.

It worked for sixteen months, give or take. He seemed to respect me and my boundaries. He pretended to be the perfect guy until the night he decided that, if I wasn't willing to give it up to him, he would just take what he thought he was owed. He used the excuse that I let him touch me. That I touched him. Why couldn't he get his dick wet? I *owed* him.

Screw that.

I managed to stop him before he went too far. I never gave him the chance to try again. I left instead.

I threw away my whole life in Connecticut, determined to start over in New Jersey without him.

So what the hell is he doing here? And since I know the answer to that question, I have a better one.

What am I supposed to do now?

CHAPTER 2
WAIT

NOX

My head is bowed forward, chin tucked to my chest, when a jolt of sudden fear shudders through my body.

Only one problem: *it's not my fear.*

Nearly every emotion but determination and a faint hope have been lost to me during my long imprisonment. Duke Haures wants to see me admit that my time with Amelia was a mistake. That I jeopardized all of Sombra out of selfishness because I couldn't stay away. But if I have a regret, it's only that my mate is out there without me to watch over her. To keep her safe.

And now she's afraid.

It's obvious. The fear rushing through my demonic body, causing the golden chains to flare in the shadows of my cage, the shine almost blinding… it settles low in my gut, lodging there in the space where I cling to my connection to my treasured Amy.

I snap to attention, chains rattling as I rise up from my slumped position against the concrete floor and cinder block wall of my dungeon cell. Fresh from bathing earlier, I'd experienced a wave of need that had me crouching in the corner, stroking the length of my cock until it was nearly raw. Since being forced to wear the golden chains that cut me almost completely off from my mate, I haven't been able to find completion in the act, though a lifetime's imprisonment in the duke's dungeons means I have more than enough time and persistence to try whenever my cock and balls grow heavy.

I've often wondered if that was Duke Haures's true punishment. Not only keeping me from my mate, but also finding any pleasure in the idea of what I might've had if I stayed away from her until the time was right to claim her.

I'm used to the need. To the desire that makes me go stiff and erect beneath my shadow-woven coverings. I'm used to the despair washing over my horns when I think of Amy existing without me, my mate on her own while I wear the chains that keep her away from both me and a fate like mine.

But fear? I was a hunter. Brave. Merciless. The only fear I've ever known was the night the duke's head soldier and his mage followed me into Amy's world and I realized that I sacrificed my future with her for one fleeting touch.

My heart is racing, though it's not *my* heart. My hands flex, then tighten, claws biting into my fleshy palms, spilling blood past my thick wrists; the same color as my red demon skin, it trickles before landing with a *plop* on the concrete beneath me. I don't know whether to run or bellow like a beast that any instinct of mine is to flee.

Only it's not *my* instinct, is it? I *feel* it, but that's only because the emotions are traveling down a mate bond that I've long tried to ignore…

It's been years. I lost track of exactly how many it's been since the promise of a mate bond became a tie that, despite the weight of the cursed chains, passes from Sombra into the human realm. The only thing that kept me sane during my imprisonment was knowing that, while I lingered in the shadows, Amy was on the other end of our bond, happy and free even if she's forgotten all about me.

But she's not happy now. Her fear is so sudden, so *stark* that I'm experiencing it in a whole other plane. Not even the golden chains controlling my shape and binding my essence are enough to dampen it which tells me that Amy is terrified.

No.

This isn't the first time I've sensed my mate. As the years passed, as she matured in a world I could no longer reach, our bond grew stronger to the point that

I had to admit it was the only thing that kept me existing in the dark, silent pit where the duke's soldiers led me after the shame of marching me in chains through my clan.

I was the cautionary tale. The evidence of the duke's might and his mercy. For breaking his first law —for being caught in my mate's quarters with no intention of bonding her to me before the next gold moon—I could've earned an execution. I didn't. He ordered me chained, and though I was strong enough to fight off the soldiers then, the cursed chains have sapped so much of my essence that I truly am a docile demon these days.

But sometimes… sometimes the veil between realms is thinner than usual. Samhain is one of them, and it usually coincides with the rising of the gold moon in Sombra. I've been getting glimpses of my human mate's emotions for days as Samhain approached, another reminder of what I had—and what I willingly gave up.

Is that why I sense her now? I don't know, and I don't care. Clutching my chest with one hand, digging into my flesh with my claws, I huff out a breath, trying to calm my racing heart.

My only thought is to get to Amy. Forget the chains. Forget the dungeon. Forget the punishment.

She is afraid. The veil between worlds is thin, and I am determined.

I dig deeper, ignoring the sting as I coat my claws

with more blood. My mate needs me, but I can not go to her while wearing the golden chains. That's the whole purpose behind them. They contain my shadows and my essence, and they make it so that I can never leave Sombra while I wear them unless another conjurer creates a portal for me.

I can't use the one that sprang up when Amy first summoned me to her. At least, not while I'm still wearing these chains, I can't. So that just means I must get rid of the chains.

Smearing my blood along the manacles on my wrists, I squeeze my fists. Then, pouring nearly every bit of essence that I have—every drop of what makes me Nox, and what I'd sacrifice for my Amy—I feed the cursed chains until the golden color has turned a blistering orange shade. They're almost molten to the touch, too, the manacles searing my skin. Gritting my teeth, gnashing my fangs, I give the chains *more*.

The chains turn black. So does my skin. For the first time since Sammael conjured the chains, I've traded my solid, red-skinned demon form for the shadowy shape that makes traveling off plane possible.

It worked. Thank the gods that it did. I hadn't thought it would, but rumors among the mages in my clan wondered if there was a way to beat the duke's punishment. They said, if the magic of the chains fed on a demon's essence bit by bit, if a prisoner allowed them to gorge on them, the chains might overload for a time. It seems as if that's true.

There's no time to question it. With a quick jerk that should've been easier than it was, I snap the length of chain in two. Now that my hands are free, I use my claws to break the manacles off. As I do, my form solidifies, going demonic again.

At least, most of it does. A thick band of black stretches around both of my wrists, a mark from where the manacles had sat before they burned me straight to the shadows.

Giving my hands a quick shake, I prowl away from the discarded chains, preparing for my next step.

I have no doubt that the chains will return. There are only two ways to be rid of them forever: with the duke's permission, or my mate's after she gives me her essence and takes me inside of her as her male. The essence of Nox will become a mixture of both Nox and Amy, and the chains won't be able to hold me anymore.

But I'm not really thinking about that now. If my mate truly is in danger—and every instinct inside of me is screaming that she is—then I must get to her. If I don't, there might not even be an Amy for me to take as mine.

No.

It won't be. It *can't* be. Amy will be safe, and I'll do everything I have to to make it so.

Starting with ripping a portal open in the middle of the duke's dungeons.

I THOUGHT I KNEW PAIN.

When I realized that I'd had my forever in my claws only to lose her because I wanted too much, too soon? My heart shattered, and I hurt.

When years passed in shadows while Amy existed in a whole other realm without me? That was a dull ache that never faded.

When I gave up most of my essence to break the chains, burning my skin down past my bone? It was excruciating, but I did it all for my mate.

But whether I gave up more than I had to spare, or the veil wasn't as thin as I thought, I don't know. Creating a portal from Sombra to the human world… as the space in front of me tore open, it was as if I did the same.

Despite giving the chains most of my essence, I recover quickly. I have to. This isn't about me. This is about getting to my mate, no matter what. So, shaking off the aftershocks of pain that have me back in my shadow form, hunched over as I jump through the portal, I do something I never thought I would again.

I cross planes into the human world.

It's dark out. With my instincts roaring at me to go right to my human mate, I didn't even think about whether I would appear in daylight—or if any other mortals would see me. Luckily, it's the time of shadows. Cold and dreary, too, with a chill in the air that sizzles against my demon skin.

I don't know where Amy is. Unlike every other time I followed a portal to her, I haven't landed in her quarters. This is the outside of the human world, with its single silver moon and an inky black sky. My bare feet are perched against a hard, rocky terrain that's so much cooler than the dusty Sombra ground. The air has a cloying, almost rotten odor that I huff through my nose as I search for my Amy's sweet scent.

Just like the night I met her as a wee child, I find a hint of it on the breeze. Nearly overpowered by the stink where I find myself, it's there—and it's coated in terror. She's still afraid, and as I sense her coming closer, I know why I've landed in this narrow pathway.

This is where Amy is heading to. And I shall be here to receive her.

Without the chains to hamper me, I immediately dissolve into mist. The faintest of my shadow forms, I back into the furthest corner of the closed-off space, hidden from any mortal that might pass by. I hover over slick yet lumpy bags littered along the side; I don't know what could be inside of them, only that they seem to be the source of the foul scent. Ignoring them, I focus on Amy.

And then, once I'm hidden, I do what I do best.

I wait.

CHAPTER 3
SHADOWS AND CLAWS

AMY

Damn it, I made a wrong turn.

The moment I locked eyes with him, I couldn't deny it. That was Connor Hart in the flesh, and though I moved to Jersey City to get away from him, somehow he found out where I ran off to. Once I realized that he was there… that as soon as he was sure it was me and he began sidling toward me, the big cat stalking his tiny mouse… I didn't even bother trying to figure it out. That would only give him more time to close the gap of the couple of blocks separating us, and I just… I couldn't allow that.

So, instead, I took off. With my purse clutched in one hand, the heavy bag of candy in the other, I turn my back on him and start to head in the opposite direction. I just needed to find a side street or an alley, some way to lose him, and then I could slip back to my apartment and find safety. Behind locked doors, I could freak out in peace—but, first, I had to get away from my stalker of an ex.

Turns out that's easier said than done.

Though I've been in Jersey City for a few months, I really don't leave my apartment much. On foot, I know where my local grocery store is, the nearby deli and convenience store, and, like, the laundromat. That's about it. The ghost of Connor always looking over my shoulder had me leaving my apartment when I had to and that was all. My neighbor made me feel like running out to get candy tonight was important, so I did, but I'm definitely regretting it now.

I'm wishing I had my car, too. I don't see Connor's parked anywhere nearby, and I might have a better chance of escaping him if I had mine.

Come on, feet. Don't fail me now.

The city looks so very different at night. Terrified out of my mind that Connor is going to grab me or something, I just go. It doesn't even occur to me to call out for help. If I know him at all—and, these days, I'm not so sure I ever did—he's not going to call attention to himself. I don't, either. Speed-walking so I look like a woman on a mission, I motor down the street, searching for the turn that would bring me back to my apartment.

But I… I miss it. I have no idea how. I guess fear

does something really wonky to a person because, next thing I know, I've crossed out of the busy street onto a vacant stretch that is eerily quiet and way too dark.

Shadows are everywhere. A handful of street lamps dot the length of the road, though more than a few of them are blacked out from shattered bulbs. Because why wouldn't they be?

Taking a deep breath, I plunge into the darkness. All I hear is the echo of my footfalls as my speed-walk turns into a bit of a jog, the bag of candy jostling against my hip. In the distance, sirens blare. My stomach goes tight at the sound, but I swallow the lump in my throat and keep on going despite how scared I am.

I never used to be afraid of the dark. As a kid, I would spend hours at night, watching the shadows play against the wall of my bedroom. After my aunt's disappearance when I was eight, my mom was worried that something would happen to me, and I spent more time in the house than most kids my age. I created friends of my own, I guess, imaginary friends who kept me company and promised that I'd always be safe.

Of course, then I grew up. The shadows were just shadows, and the dark lost any of the magic it once had. My Aunt Su never came back from where she vanished off to, and though my mom was still frightened that she could lose me, too, she had to let me live my life.

Not that I really did, apart from going to college and trying to get my business off the ground—until I met Connor. Or, rather, Connor met *me*… and, in the last year, I discovered that the dark could be a very, very scary place indeed.

Connor likes to whistle.

It's a silly little habit he has. He told me once that he doesn't like quiet, so he found a way to fill it. I thought it was charming at first. He would sit on the couch next to me, guiding my head to rest on his shoulder as I read my book and he whistled a different melody each time.

But then he began to grow annoyed if I ignored him too long. He'd pluck my book from my hand, tossing it across the room. His gentle cuddles turned into groping that I would find any reason to avoid. The best way was for me to suggest we play "name that tune." He would whistle, and I'd have to guess what song it was.

The night he decided he didn't want to wait for me anymore, he whistled Britney Spears's "I'm a Slave 4 U". After everything that happened to the pop star earlier this year, her music seems to be everywhere again, just like it was when I was a senior in high school. I actually stopped listening to Z100 because just hearing those iconic opening notes had me flashing back to the night Connor tried cornering me in my bedroom.

It's a different song tonight. Still, like Pavlov's freaking dog, the second I hear him begin to whistle, I react.

First, I glance behind me, but I don't see him. Good. That means I have some time to hide. Dashing forward, I drop down into a crouch beside a dark car parked along the empty street. I'm positioned perfectly between two lamp posts so I'm tucked in the shadows. Unless he walks over here, he'll never see me.

The whistle grows closer. Over the thump of my heart, I recognize the melody. Almost without meaning to, I start singing along in my head.

… never gonna give you up…

Oh, god.

Clamping my trembling hand over my mouth, I force back my whimper. Because I know that song—just like I know why he's picked it to whistle right now.

I'm not so internet savvy. I have a Myspace from shortly after I finished college that I spent one long weekend decorating with glitter and .gifs before never logging in again. I use my computer for working toward getting my business off the ground, printing out Mapquest directions, and looking up movie times—and, honestly, that's about all.

Not Connor. He has an obsession with something called 4chan that I never really understood. But I do know about their fascination with this new meme thing called "rickrolling". You play a video when, suddenly, it's an old '80s song by Rick Astley. "Never Gonna Give You Up". He got a kick out of tricking me into watching the redhead in the tan trench coat sing an upbeat ballad while he hummed—and, yes, whistled—along.

It was our song, he told me. His promise to me. No matter what, he was never going to give me up.

And now he's out there, whistling the tune while I huddle alongside a parked car, trying to figure out how to escape him.

Did I think I was scared shitless before? That's nothing compared to now.

He's going to find me. I'm trapped like a sitting duck, and if I don't get out of here, he's going to find me—and there's no one around to stop him like last time. If my mom hadn't come home earlier than expected, if she hadn't knocked on my bedroom door when she had… I don't know what would've happened.

But I have a pretty good idea what Connor plans on doing if he gets his hands on me now.

Oh, he says he just wants to explain. I've heard that a hundred times before. He wants to apologize, to explain, to show me what I'm missing out on. We spent a year-and-a-half together. I shouldn't throw that all away because of the one time he couldn't control himself.

Yeah freaking *right.*

I told him in the beginning. I said he was wasting his time with me, that he was expecting something I might not ever be able to give him. He was the one who was convinced that we were meant to be.

Three months after I told him we were over, he still hasn't given up. But now I know exactly how far he'll go to get what he wants.

And he wants me.

Shit.

My bags dragging against the sidewalk, I crawl on my hands and knees, still hiding behind the side of the car as I try to put some distance between us.

It's not enough.

"Amy…" Connor's sing-song voice sends a shiver up and down my spine. It's better than the whistle, but barely. "Come out, come out wherever you are."

No way in hell. Tucking the bags under my arms, trying desperately to stop the plastic from rustling, I crawl another foot forward.

Looking back, I should've just abandoned the candy. I could always buy more, and it wasn't worth signaling to Connor where I was. But I didn't, and when the bag slips from my hold, hitting the sidewalk with a *thud*, I can't swallow the curse that pops out fast enough.

Connor chuckles. Because of course he does. He's *winning*.

"Stop being ridiculous. I know you're here. Come on, darling. I just want to talk."

Darling… I never knew anyone who could take such a term of endearment and turn it into a threat like Connor does.

He sounds closer. The last thing I need is for him to catch up to me while I'm sprawled on the asphalt so, tapping into the tiny bit of self-preservation I have left, I rise up to my knees and glance over the trunk of the car.

Connor has one hand tucked in his pocket, thumb casually strumming his belt loop. He's strolling on the inside of the street, assured that no one will interrupt him as he eases his way toward me. Beneath the moonlight, I can see his big grin. And in his other hand? He's gripping something that looks dark and bulky.

Maybe it's his cell phone. Maybe it's a weapon. Maybe it's a fucking rock, I don't know, but my heart sinks all the way to my shoes when I notice his hand isn't empty. Call it a gut reaction. Whatever he has… it's not good.

I still have a slight lead. Not much, but I don't think he ever expected me to run. Honestly, I wouldn't put it past my cocky, obsessive ex to believe that, eventually, he'd snap his fingers and I'd simply obey.

Not in this lifetime.

Hopping up to my feet, barely aware that I'm still clutching the bag of candy and my purse, I take off again. No speed-walking for me this time. It's a flat-out sprint.

Behind me, Connor calls my name, but I don't pay him any attention. If he really wanted me to believe that his intentions were innocent, he'd let me go. He'd give me my space, and maybe try to contact me again when I wasn't visibly panicking.

He doesn't.

Instead, he laughs. The bane of my existence, and he *laughs*.

"Go right ahead, darling. You want to see if I'll chase? I thought I proved to you I would, but that's alright. I'll get you."

And then the prick starts to whistle Blondie's "One Way or Another" as he starts to jog after me.

His arrogance is on my side. So sure that he'll catch up to me, he doesn't expect that I'll do anything to escape. Like, oh, following my gut again and heading toward a side street coming up on my left?

I bolt toward the darkness, hoping like hell that there will be somewhere to hide in there. Maybe a back exit to a storefront that wouldn't mind concealing me, or a dumpster that Connor would never guess I'd be desperate enough to hop into.

But I am. I totally am.

He thinks he's the good guy. That's what makes this so awful. He doesn't see anything wrong with all that he's done. Between what happened back in Madison, or how he promised that he'd never let me go when I first tried to break up with him… in Connor's warped brain, I'm playing a game of "hard to get" and he's just trying his best to win.

Like any winner, if he gets his hands on me, he'll want his prize. And Connor has made it clear that the only thing he wants is *me*. He wants me in his bed, in his life, and he won't stop until he gets everything he thinks he deserves.

I escaped him once. He won't let me get away again. He said as much in the hundreds of texts and voicemails he left for me before I traded my Nokia cell phone for one of those pay-as-you-go phones I bought just to keep in touch with my mom. Maybe he was drunk as he later claimed, or maybe the real Connor was finally coming out from behind his charming smile and boyish good looks, but he told me that if he couldn't have me, no one could.

I believe him, too.

The second I step into the alley, I stop short. I can't help it. Not only is it pitch black, but there's a layer of fog that wasn't out there on the empty street. It seems to hover, luring me in, and scared as I am… it feels like I should.

Something's off about it, too. In the middle of the urban center, a few twisted, gnarled, winter-bare trees are rising up along the edge of the brick siding. Both sides, too, like a haunted, hazy forest has been picked up and dropped on the secret side street in Jersey City.

What the—

And that's when a pair of glowing red eyes appear in the darkness, and suddenly I'm nine again, with the gleaming gaze of a bogeyman watching me from the shadows of my bedroom.

I'm ten, and Nox isn't just made of shadows. He's a shadow man, a solemn demon who talks to me in a harsh language that I work hard to learn.

I'm eleven, and the book that Aunt Su left behind before she disappeared is missing from my room. I'd memorized the foreign words—the *verus amor* spell that first brought Nox to my world—but I was afraid I'd forget them and my shadow man would never visit me again. But he does, and I only feel safe when he's there, watching over me until I go to sleep.

I'm twelve, and hiding under my bed because Nox told me to. Other demons, just like him, are in my room, and they put chains on Nox before dragging him out of my life forever. Before long, he's just a dream, and I'm back to being lonely Amy again.

I'm twenty-six, and all those memories of my imaginary friend seem suddenly real. I'd honestly thought they were dreams—I thought they were *fantasies*—but I'd convinced myself that Nox was just someone I made up.

And yet… I know those eyes. The way the shadows reach for me, a warm breeze that caresses my skin. The pull I feel toward the silhouette looming in the distance… and, most importantly, that rasp of a voice as he says one word.

"*Run.*"

It's not in English. The actual syllable he says is closer to "corr", but I translate it instantly. He just said "run"—but I know without being able to explain how that he isn't talking to me.

Turning to glance behind me, I gasp. Connor is standing at the entrance to the alleyway, staring at me. For a heartbeat, I'm not sure if he can see Nox's red eyes peering at him from the other side, but then he gestures to me wildly.

"Amy, get over here." The humor is gone from his voice. He actually sounds as shaky as I feel. "Right the fuck now."

"No," comes the rumbling voice from the shadows. "Amelia… come to me."

Peering into the darkness, I can just about make out his shape. Reaching out of the swirling shadows, he crooks an inky black claw at me.

A… a claw. That's a *claw*.

Nox had claws. I know because I always wondered if they would be sharp. Not that I ever thought he'd cut me—I didn't—but, like everything else when it came to the shadow man, I was curious.

Come to me…

Something tells me that, if I walk into those shadows, I'm not walking out of them again. At least, not as the same person I was going in.

Does that stop me?

Not even a little.

When it comes to either facing Connor behind me or the truth that my childhood dreams are real, I know exactly which one I'm choosing.

I dash for my shadow monster.

CHAPTER 4
RUN

NOX

As a Sombra demon, we know our mates instinctively. One look in her eyes and we're lost to the sensation that we're gazing at our forever.

I did when I first met my Amy. Only, because she was so young, I recognized who she would eventually be to me in time. When she matured, she'd be my mate, and I looked forward to watching her blossom into her beauty.

But that was many human years ago. And though I don't know quite how many have passed, there's no denying that she's more lovely than I ever would've imagined.

She's grown taller, though still so very delicate compared to my demon strength and size. No horns, of course, and her pale skin seems almost translucent in the weak moonlight. Her hair cascades in dark waves down her back; I'm no good with colors, not like the artists in the clan, but it reminds me of the dry dirt on the edge of Nuit where it's red mingled with black. Brown, I think she told me it was called.

And her body… if I had any doubt in my mind that my Amy is a mature female, her body proves that she is. Not only is she taller, but she's wider, too, with hips begging for me to take them beneath my claws, and breasts I'd give my left horn to see without any of her human coverings on. From her panicked flight, they're rising and falling, the low cut of her covering revealing cleavage that has my cock stirring.

No, Nox, I tell myself. She's my mate, yes, but taking her is only second to saving her. She's frightened, and while I may be a male, I strive to be honorable when I can. I must protect her. Only then may I earn the chance to hold her close.

Especially since it's another male that is causing her to be so scared.

He appears at the edge of my shadows a few moments after Amy finds me. Trapped between us, my mate is peering at me while I hunger to hunt down the threat to her.

I bare my fangs, though he can't see me through the thicket of my shadows. He thinks he's a predator? I'll show him what a true monster can be.

Because it's clear to me what happened: a

human male has chased *my* mate through the dark of night. It doesn't matter to me who he is or why he thinks he has any claim to Amy. She's fated to a Sombra demon which means that, human or not, *I* am her mate. Her place is with me, and only because I don't know exactly what kind of relationship she has with this male do I spare him.

And… that's not quite true. If she'd gone to him when he called her, I don't know what I would've done. But she doesn't. As if she recognizes who her true mate is, I crook my claw at her, and she joins me in my shadows.

She takes my hand. Only our second touch, this time it does what it could not while she was still spawn. Her icy fingers pressed against mine, our mate bond snaps into place.

Amy stumbles. The male takes advantage of her misstep to edge toward my shadows.

I refuse to let him.

"Go now," I snarl, tucking Amy behind me. She's trembling against my back, her small form pressed to my side, and I've never felt more powerful. She chose *me*. "Run, human."

It's the same command I gave before. In Sombran, of course, but it doesn't matter that the human wouldn't know my language. The meaning is clear in any tongue. Either that, or the way I part the shadows just enough to reveal a hint of my shadow form. I'm not supposed to let anyone see me, but I risk it to send the human male running.

He does. With only a yelp as an answer, he leaves Amy to me while fleeing like the most skittish of prey.

Coward. He does not know that I am Amy's mate, or that a Sombra demon would rather face chains or execution than hurt their female. He just fled from her, leaving her behind with me.

I drift away, staying in my shadow form as I gesture toward the empty alley. I want her to see that I've made the male leave.

But Amy… she doesn't follow the point of my claw. Instead, dropping the totes she has in each of her hands, she moves toward me. Our skin doesn't touch again—I make sure of it, though it's hard—as she stares up at me.

"Is this real?" she whispers. "I thought… you left me. I never thought I'd see you again. Oh, Nox… I can't believe this is happening. That you're *here*."

It's her human language. English. I recognize the strange syllables, so soft and lyrical compared to the harsh sounds that make up Sombran, but I don't know what she said. I used to understand a little. That was before, though. Before I spent many human years in solitude, where even Sombran lost some of its meaning to me.

I shake my head, the same sign I used when we first met and she slipped into English during another one of her excited rants. I'd listen to her voice forever

—just as I'd stare down at her beauty for equally as long—but I have no idea what she said.

Except for my name. She said my name.

"I am Nox," I tell her. "I am yours."

Her mouth moves, though she doesn't make any sound this time. Amy's smooth brow furrows, hair falling forward to shield her gorgeous face from me. I already touched her once, the mate bond igniting between us, but until she accepts my offer, I can't dare touch her again.

She must want my essence. I can't force it on her. It must be her choice.

It seems like an eternity, but it's mere seconds before she nods. Then, as if it took her a moment to find the words, she says in broken Sombran, "I thought you were a fantasy."

Fantasy? Ah. It must be an inexact translation from her human language to mine. When Sammael stayed behind to erase me from my mate's memories, he said his magic would make it so that I was naught but a dream to her.

Only I'm real, and so is she.

She has one arm folded around her middle, tote hanging at her side, her expression suddenly lost and helpless. My stomach goes tight, sure that I'm the reason she looks like she doesn't know what to do next… but then I realize something.

The male is gone, and so is the fear tinging her scent.

"I am no fantasy. I am Nox," I repeat.

"I know. I remember." Amy tips her head back after another moment, meeting my unblinking stare again. "You… you told Connor to run."

Connor. The male who chased my mate right to me. While I finally have her where she belongs—at my side—that doesn't change the fact that she was still frightened before. He was the one who had scared her, and I wonder if I should have done more than send him scampering off like that.

"I did." I have to fold my claws into fists to keep from stroking her pale skin. "I thought you wanted him to go."

Did I make a mistake? The Amy I remember was inquisitive and demanding, yet also gentle and kind. If she wanted me to, I would hunt the male down—but I thought she'd prefer him to leave instead.

She nods.

I gulp. "Do you… do you want me to go?"

I can already sense the mate bond at work. Beneath my shadow coverings, my cock is stirring once more. I forced it to go down and stay limp while I thought about how frightened my mate was, but as her sweet scent envelopes me… I want nothing more than to claim my Amy here and now.

If she was a demoness, I would. She'd be experiencing the mate bond the same as I am, her instincts leading her to forget her fright and cleave to me. But she's human, and different in so many ways.

I hold my breath as I wait for my mate to answer me.

Amy shakes her head. "I don't want to be alone," she whispers. "Don't leave me again."

Nothing on this plane or Sombra could make me. Not even Duke Haures or his dreaded chains will force me to abandon my mate again. She's a mature female now, my body recognizing her instinctively as my own true mate, and I refuse to be separated from her. Unless she tells me to go, I'll be with her—and, as soon as she's willing to accept me, I'll make her mine for the rest of our long lives.

I gave her the chance to refuse me. I gave her the opportunity to tell me to leave because, gods know, I don't have the strength in me to do so myself.

Now my Amy is as good as mine, and if I have to keep her safe in my shadows until she's my bonded mate, I will. There's only one way to do that, though. I can hide her, but to do that, I need to give her my essence.

I need to start the mating rituals, including the mate's promise. But first—

She's in my shadows, but she's not a part of them. Not yet. Only when I give her my essence will I be able to shield her from any mortal's sight. Especially since I expect that male might return for Amy—because, gods know, I would—I must do what I can to keep her hidden.

And once I have her, no one… not her male, not

the duke, not his soldiers… can make me let her go. Only Amy herself, and even then I'm not so sure I'd be able to do so willingly…

Reaching down, I snag her hand in mine. A quick touch. Fleeting, because her skin is icy compared to mine and I don't want to burn her. Once she has my essence and I have hers, our temperatures will be compatible, but until then I must be careful. With a layer of shadows buffering our bodies, I press her palm to my chest, laying her white fingers over my heart.

"Do you trust me?" I ask her.

The child I knew trusted me implicitly. The female before me… I'm not so sure she will, and I swallow a sigh of relief when she slowly bobs her head up and down.

"You saved me again. When I needed you the most, you came back. Do I trust you? Of course I do."

That's all I needed to hear. I hold out my hand again. Without even a moment's hesitation, she places her tiny one in mine.

I shudder and, bowing my head, I give her all the essence I have left.

Everything I am. Everything I was. Everything I'll ever be… it belongs to Amelia Benoit now. She'll know everything about me, and though I wish I could spare her the time I spent in the duke's dungeons, if she doesn't search for those memories, she'll never have to know what I experienced. She can just sense my love for her, my longing, and how devoted I've always been to my mate.

She hasn't given me her essence yet. I haven't asked for it, and so long as we save our mate's promise for when we fully bond, I shouldn't have to worry about my Amy suffering from mate sickness. For the moment, at least, I can wrap her up in my shadows, content that the chains won't stop me from holding her close.

She's mine. She always has been, and now that she's here, I will do my best to make sure she understands that.

Even if I have to steal her to my shadows to make it so.

CHAPTER 5
ESSENCE AND NEED

AMY

I gasp. I don't mean to, but I can't help it.

The hand holding mine was made up of inky black shadows with claws arcing over the tips of his long, thin fingers. He was careful not to cut me with them, squeezing my hand gently as something passed between us. For a split second, his skin—which was tangible despite being shadow—went incredibly hot. It was almost like I stuck my hand in a flame, but the sensation was over before I could jerk it back.

That's when I see that his has changed. It's completely solid now. The skin is a deep red shade, almost like rust, though he has a dark black mark around three inches wide surrounding his wrist. His claws are just as black, and I can feel the points digging into the back of my hand now.

I don't snatch it away because I'm afraid it'll force Nox to slice me open. Instead, I glance up—and then I stare.

I remember Nox. Whether I believed he was real until now or not, I do remember him. And there's a reason why I call him the shadow man—or the shadow monster—in my head. He's always had two forms that I knew of: the hulking black shadow with high, curving horns, his claws, his fangs, and the blazing red eyes serving as the only spot of color on him, and a nearly invisible mist for when he melted so completely into the shadows around him that I sensed his presence more than saw him. That form was both transparent and intangible, as if he was a ghost, and it's how he was able to hide on the handful of occasions my mom peeked her head in my room when she wondered who the hell I was talking to.

But this Nox… he's different.

It isn't just his hands that are red. His whole body is. The shadows have faded, leaving a true monster in their place. I can see every detail of him, from the sharp planes of his shockingly different if undeniably attractive face, the contours of his incredibly muscular body, and his full seven—*seven*—and-a-half-foot height. He has stick-straight black hair that hits his hard jaw, ridges over his long, pointed nose, fangs curving over his bottom lips… and his horns. They're polished and somehow even larger.

You know, I used to be so fascinated by his onyx horns. Almost as much as his brilliant red eyes…

He's huge, more than two feet taller than me, though he hunches slightly as if trying to make himself smaller. I can guess why. He probably thinks I'm horrified at this appearance of his I've never seen before. And, yeah, it's a shock. Not gonna lie about that. I'd always wondered if he was hiding something in the shadows, and now… now I can say for sure that, uh, yeah. He is.

His eyes are still a burning red color, much brighter than the duller shade of his skin. They've dimmed some as I run my gaze over him, taking him in, and when I see that his expression is closed-off as if he's expecting me to freak out or something, I look away.

I look *down*.

And… whoa.

There's about a foot separating us right now. He's still holding my hand in a loose grasp, but he's keeping the rest of his body away from mine which makes it pretty obvious to see what he's packing down below.

He's naked. No shirt. No shoes. No pants. In this more demon form, he's got not a stitch of shadow to wrap around him, and I get my first peek at Nox's cock.

And, oh, mama…

It's freaking huge. Obviously. I mean, guys are

usually pretty proportionate in size, right? I guess he could have had, like, a hot dog or something swinging between his meaty, thick thighs, but he definitely doesn't. It's hard, the base of his shaft a deep red while the head is almost purple. It's nudging his groin, tickling the black curls nestled there, and if I ever stopped to think if demons had pubes, I sure as heck know the answer now.

I shouldn't stare. Barely a couple of minutes ago, I was so scared that Connor might try to force me to touch him that I ran blindly into an alley full of shadows rather than face him. But now my imaginary friend is here, he's *real,* and he's visibly aroused.

And I can't take my eyes off of that monster dick.

As I stare, he eases his hand out of mine. "Amelia?"

"Amy," I whisper. It's a knee-jerk reaction. Hearing my full name makes me feel like I'm in trouble—and Nox should know that. As a petulant child, if he called me 'Amelia', I stuffed my fingers in my ears until he relented and said 'Amy' instead.

Hey. It was better than 'spawn'…

Oof.

You know how you can have a memory in the back of your brain and, without meaning to, another innocent thought or smell or something can unlock it? That happened to me right then. If you'd asked me ten minutes ago about Nox, I would've whole-heartedly believed he was a figment of my imagination, a shadow man I made up because of my traumatic childhood. In one summer, my aunt went missing, my mother and father got divorced, and I moved from New Haven to Madison to be close in case Aunt Su came back. We traded our big house for a two-bedroom apartment where I lived with Mom until I finally left for Jersey City a couple of months ago, and my world was in turmoil. Of course I created an imaginary friend who was devoted to watching over me, protecting me, and keeping me both company and safe.

But that was ten minutes ago.

Now?

Just thinking the word 'spawn' sparks a whole bunch of suppressed memories. Because that's what he used to call me. In an almost teasing grunt, the translation for 'kid' and 'child' in Sombran was basically 'spawn' and he always said it with affection. I'd hated him using that term on me—even more than 'Amelia'—and when he did, I called him 'monster' back which he wasn't too happy with. He was a proud Sombra demon, after all.

That's not all it sparks, though. As if, somehow, Nox has crawled into my brain, I know instinctively his reason behind it. He had to remind himself that I was young. That I wasn't mature.

That I wasn't ready to be his mate…

But I am now. I've grown up, and it isn't just because I'm a woman, he's a man—a *male*—and we're standing so close that he's so obviously hard. It's because he's known since the moment I read that page in my aunt's old book that I would grow up and be his fated mate.

He wants to fuck me. And I don't just think that because of his state. I *know* it because I suddenly understand what a mate means to a Sombra demon. They only get one, one female that they can sleep with, that they can procreate with, that they can spend the rest of their immortal life with.

And that's supposed to be *me*.

It's one thing to be entranced when I got my first look at Nox both naked and erect. I've seen porn. I know Connor's cock better than I ever wanted to. I've had my hands and mouth on his, hoping that that would be enough to keep him from pushing me for sex, so it's not like I'm some innocent virgin scandalized at seeing her first dick.

Just the opposite actually. With my ex, I had to work up the stomach to be physical with him. With Nox… my first instinct is to reach out and see if I can wrap my hand around the girth of his massive cock. With Nox's thoughts in my head, the only one Amy can pull together is this: I've never let a guy put his dick inside of me before, so I'm not so sure that we'll fit—but I kinda want to give Nox a try.

Holy shit.

The fact that I have the insane urge to do that has me taking my hand back and scooting a few steps away from him. Finally remembering that I've got my beat-up bag of Halloween candy hanging from the crook of one arm, my purse hanging off my other wrist, I drop it all to the asphalt before wrapping my arms around my midsection.

I have to. If I don't, I might lunge forward and satisfy my sudden curiosity about whether his shaft is as hot as the rest of him or not.

Meeting his gaze, I see that his expression is still guarded. Does he know that *I* know what he's thinking? When he touched me… something happened. I can't quite pinpoint what, but he asked me if I trusted him, and then he did something that plugged me right into him.

And, oh jeez, now I have this desire to plug his cock right into *me*.

I don't know what's going on, but I have to ask.

"What… what did you just do to me?"

I'm speaking in Sombran. That's not a surprise. Back when I knew him, Nox was content to keep our conversations in his demon language because I was so eager to learn it for him. Before, I had to struggle to remember it—mainly because that was something else I convinced myself I made up—but, like riding a bike, once I flexed that muscle in my brain, I could call up the words. Stilted, sure, but I could talk to him again.

Now, after whatever he did, I'm changed. Instead of speaking Sombran as a second language, it's like I instinctively know every nuance of Nox's tongue—almost as if it's mine.

How the—

Nox, as ever, proves he might be a demon, but he's a smart one. He doesn't even try to deny that he did *something* to me.

Tilting his chin up enough to give him a roguish air, he says, "I gave you my essence."

Huh? "I'm sorry. Your *what*? And why? Why did you do that?"

He looks at me like I should already know the answer. And… hang on… I do.

Essence. Every living creature has it. In English, the closest translation would be 'soul'. I was right when I said that something passed between us. He actually transferred a piece of his soul into me so that I could be protected by his shadows. At least, that's part of the reason. With his essence, I now know everything there is to know about him, and protecting me is absolutely his first priority.

But a Sombra demon male can only give his essence away to one person: his true mate.

And Nox finally confirms that everything I suddenly know is correct when he swallows roughly and says, "Because you're my mate."

MATE.

Boom.

Mate.

Boom.

The one word in his raspy voice is repeating on a loop in my poor brain as I stare up at him again. He refuses to look away, as though he's been thinking of seeing me again in the years since we've been separated and is waiting for me to disappear again.

But I'm not the one who left him. He left me because… because—

As his memories rise up, I shake my head. I'm not ready to deal with that. It doesn't matter why Nox had to go. He's here now, he's telling me I'm his mate, and I… I'm surprisingly okay with that.

I mean, it kinda makes sense. My whole life, I've never been attracted to another person. Like, I could appreciate when another woman was gorgeous or when a guy was a hottie, but I never thought, "Gee, I'd like to get them naked."

I figured I was asexual. I had some romantic feelings—even for Connor—but the idea of sex with anyone repulsed me going back to puberty. Making out made me nauseous, and whenever I was intimate with Connor, I ran the plot of the most recent romance novel I read through my head just to fake some sense of arousal for him. And when that didn't work? I had a foolproof fantasy that I have never, ever admitted out loud before.

I knew I was different from the time I was in

middle school and my friends were all giggling, trying to get the boys'—and some girls'—attention. Not me. I just thought I was a late bloomer, that it was a phase, and one that took me right through my first year of college.

That's when one of my roommates put on an old movie one night after a long week of exams. It was *Legends* with Tom Cruise and Tim Curry, and while my girlfriends all swooned over Jack, I couldn't help but think that Darkness was more my type.

I want to blame the movie. But, truth be told, ever since I was old enough to at least wonder what sex would be like, a red-skinned, horned devil-type monster has had a starring role in my fantasies for way longer than I wanted to admit. He didn't look *exactly* like the character from the movie. His face was less swarthy, and he had a sexy rumble that sounds just like Nox does. His horns arced up and back instead of forward, and though his skin was red, so were my fantasy man's eyes.

Because it was Nox. No denying it now that I've finally seen what he looks like when he isn't made up of shadows.

Holy shit. I've been dreaming of banging *Nox* for as long as I can remember.

And I had no idea because I'd never seen this side of him—until right this very moment.

Is it because I'm his mate? How long has he known that we were fated? I get the sense that he knew the instant we met—and that's why he had to constantly remind himself I was too young. From his memories, I can see that he's not a perv or anything—he didn't start to stroke that giant dick off to thoughts of me until years after he was gone—but now…

I'm not the only one itching to grab his hard cock and play with it.

So why not? Why shouldn't we? Glancing behind me for a moment, I check to make sure that the alley is as empty as it was after Nox scared Connor off. If I thought that the foggy, thick shadows filling the alley before were dense, that's nothing compared to now. Sure, it's dark, but I can see Nox just fine. It's like the rest of the world is hidden from my sight.

Oh. Right. It is. Or, better yet, I'm hidden from the world. As soon as I allowed him to give me his essence, the same trust I showed him allowed him to hide me in his shadows.

Connor won't see me. Neither will anybody who might pass the alley by… but I'm mainly worried about Connor. It's just me and Nox, and as the last of the fear I was feeling before simply fades away, I realize something.

I'm not scared, but I'm freaking *hot*.

My skin is pins and needles. My boobs are chafing against my bra. My belly has gone tight, and when I squeeze my legs together, I gasp at how sensitive my pussy is all of a sudden.

Not just sensitive. *Achy*. It needs attention, and if it doesn't get it, it's almost like I'm about to hurl.

Again, what the freaking—

Nox's head snaps toward me. His nostrils flare, and the groan that escapes him makes it clear that his demon senses are as powerful now as they used to be when I was a kid. He could always tell me how I was feeling by scent alone, and if that's still true? He's gotta know I'm more aroused than I've ever been before.

Glancing down again, I watch as his cock twitches. He bats it with the back of his hand, and I dart out my tongue, dabbing the corner of my mouth.

What would it taste like? Going down on Connor was a chore I had to get through, but Nox… I have to admit I'm curious.

My shadow man knows, but while I'm already trying to figure out how I can seduce him as a way to say 'hello, nice to see you again', he has more pressing concerns on his mind.

Hiding in his shadows, I'm not worried about Connor at the moment.

Nox is.

"My essence will protect you," he tells me in a rough voice, fangs on display, "and my shadows will conceal you. I want nothing more than to learn you all over again, my mate, but it must wait. The human male is still a threat. Let me take care of it, then I shall return to you."

No. That's not what's supposed to happen. I'm his mate. He… he came for me. He saved me.

Fuck Connor. He's probably in his car, speeding back toward Connecticut right now. And I need… I need Nox. As crazy as it sounds, the idea of him going any further away from me that he has just seems *wrong*.

Like something bad could happen.

"You're leaving me? You can't."

"I must."

Fine. "Then let me go with you."

Sure, the shadows are thick, but I won't feel safe if my monster goes and I stay behind. And what if he goes back to Sombra and I never see him again? Worse, what if Connor really did have a weapon in his hand?

Nox shakes his head. "It's better if you don't. I won't allow him to scare you again, but I also don't want to scare you myself. A hunt's not always pretty."

You know what? I appreciate that. I really do. I also know exactly how Nox would stop Connor from coming after me again, and as much as I wish that he left me alone, I can't stand here and let Nox hunt Connor down. Because he would. He's always been fierce, brave, and enticingly dangerous to me… and that was before I had his essence. He totally would track Connor like prey—and I can't let that happen.

That's my soft-hearted side. I'm also selfish. He tells me that I'm his mate, and his body is obviously primed to go. I've never wanted to know what sex was like so bad in my life. We're mates, right? Fated mates. He's spent his whole life waiting for me, and I just discovered that I'm his.

Maybe… maybe I could use that to convince him to stay.

"Please, Nox," I say, and if I sound like I'm begging, that's probably because I am. "I… I need you."

He was already preparing to move past me, determined to track down Connor, but he goes immovably still when I call his name.

Nox swallows. "Need me?" he echoes. "For what?"

That's the thing. I'm not really sure how to explain.

I step next to him. Something tells me to touch him, and when I lay my hand on his elbow, the nearest part of him that I can reach? The wave of relief that slams into me is just enough proof that I'm not making it up. I need him badly.

"What is it, my Amy?" His brow furrows, making the ridges over his nose more prominent. "Is it the mate sickness? But it shouldn't affect you… you haven't given me your essence."

Is he so sure about that? I was a kid who gave more of who I am to my shadow man than anyone else I ever knew. Even now he's been playing a starring role in my adult fantasies.

Mate sickness… tapping into Nox, I know what that is. When two mates share a bond and their essence, but they haven't finalized their mating by letting the male shoot his load inside of his female, the unbroken bond urges them to get down to it.

I'm not kidding when I tell him that I need him to touch me. I think… I think I need him to do more than that.

"I feel so empty," I confess. "And, oh god… is this what it's like to be horny? I need you, Nox. Please… don't go."

"Never," he vows, throwing open his arms. "I will never leave you again."

CHAPTER 6
HIS REASON

AMY

Taking the invitation for what it is, I move into him. The second I wrap my arms around his naked waist, it's like I've sunk into an ice bath. The warmth fades—which is amazing because Nox is already on fire—and the nausea rushing through me immediately disappears.

Too bad the urge to rub myself all over him like a cat in heat only ratchets up to eleven.

So I do. I barely even realize that I am, but I shift my hips, straddling his thigh so that I can start rubbing my pussy on him. I still have my jeans and panties on, giving me some friction, but I'm already so turned on that I'm seconds away from going off like a rocket.

I still feel empty, though. And, keening softly, the need going to my head, I whisper that to Nox as I lay my head between his pecs, squeezing his thigh between both of mine. "This is good, but it's not enough. I need more. I need *you*."

Call it instinct. Call it a fantasy come to life. I've never been closer to grabbing a dick and working it inside of me until this very second, and I only hope that—as my mate—Nox is as ready to fuck me as I am him.

Only he's not, and he sounds full of regret as he rejects me gently.

"And I wish I could give you everything you desire. But I can not."

Okay. So he isn't ready. That's fair. With my history, I'm the last one to try to push someone to do something they don't want to. Immediately I try to put some space between us but, before I can pull away from him, he grips my neck, keeping me clinging to him.

"I want to. Don't misunderstand me. I want you desperately, my Amy, but I can't mate you now," rumbles Nox. The vibrations coming from his chest just about caress my cheek. "You deserve silk. At the least, you deserve bedding instead of—"

"Garbage," I supply for him. He's got a point. "I guess you're right. I probably don't want my first time having sex to be in a dirty, garbage-filled alley."

Especially since Connor could come back any minute…

I didn't even realize what it was that I said until Nox exhales softly, his warm breath fluttering my flyaways.

"You waited for me," he breathes out. "You waited for your male… ah, my mate. When I saw the human… he never touched you?"

If I tell Nox that Connor did, I'm not so sure I can stop him from going after him again. Not because I was intimate with him—I can sense through this tie between us that Nox is pleased I'm still a virgin, though it wouldn't have changed a thing if I wasn't—but because he touched me in ways I never wanted.

If he has any of my essence, it's not enough for him to know everything about me the way I do him. I'll take that as a small win for the moment. If Connor comes back, I'll have to tell Nox, but that's a problem for tomorrow.

Tonight's problem is trying to figure out how I can convince Nox to do something to slake this lust I'm suffering from.

"Not like that," I tell him honestly. "I never wanted him to."

"And I… you're willing to allow me to come inside you?"

Mate sickness or whatever this is, it turns Amy into a wanton. Or maybe it's the way his voice goes impossibly deeper as he cups the back of my neck, trailing his fingers along my throat. It doesn't matter. My answer is the same regardless.

"*Yes.*"

"You know I never—"

I nod. "I know. It's alright. We'll figure this out together."

"I can't mate you at this moment, but if you'd let me… mate sickness is cured by a touch. The more intimate, the better." Nox lifts his hand. From his wrist down, it's shadow. "I would touch you, if I could."

Touch you…

"Where?" I ask, more breathlessly than I mean to.

Slipping his hand between our bodies, he pats his thigh before using his claws to scratch at the front of my jeans. As a shadow, they're blunted. I can sense his touch—and, oh, does it feel good—but it's softer than when he's in his demon form.

He could touch my pussy and not scratch me. That's what he's showing me.

And I'm more than willing to let him try.

Climbing off of his thigh, I take a step back, reaching for the button on my jeans. Once I do, once I start to tug the zipper down, Nox strokes the top of my hand, then gently pushes it away.

"Let me," he grunts. "I've waited a long time to be able to touch you. I won't miss a moment of it."

Um. Okay, then.

I drop my trembling hands to my sides. Nox leans

over me, wrapping one arm around my waist, tugging me against him. My back is pressed to his chest now, and through my hoodie, I feel his scorching heat on my back. October on the East Coast is hit or miss. I've seen snow by Halloween, and I've spent the holiday in a heavy costume that had me sweating to death. When I left to head to the convenience store earlier, I thought my zip-up hoodie and jeans would be enough, and it would've been for a quick trip.

I never expected to run into Connor—and then, well, *run.* It's grown colder in the hour or so since, but Nox is so hot, he's keeping me nice and toasty. Even as he starts to shimmy my jeans down past my ass, his hands leave a brand on my hip that warms me to the core.

"What's this?" he murmurs, more to himself than me. His claw slips under the waistband of my underwear.

I swallow. "Do demonesses not wear panties?"

"Is that what this scrap is called?"

Huh. It is a scrap, isn't it? "Yes."

"Then I wouldn't know. You are the first female… the only female… I've ever seen undress."

Because I wasn't already a sure thing before? That… that right there seals it.

My need has only grown since he looped his arm around me so that he has full access to my body. Once he's tugged my panties down to my knees, Nox lowers himself to the street. As if I weigh nothing at all, he maneuvers me so that my back is still tucked to his chest, one arm hooked behind his neck with my legs resting on his thighs in an M-shape. They're as spread as they can be with my jeans and panties still wrapped around my knees, but Nox doesn't seem to have any trouble finding my pussy.

We both groan as he uses two fingers to glide through my folds. I don't think I realized just how wet I was until he finds no resistance before he reaches my clit and, oh my God, I squirm.

My demon is strong, though. He holds me tightly, keeping me right where he wants me as his exploring becomes just a little more possessive.

It feels freaking *amazing*.

"So soft." He shudders beneath me. "I never expected you'd be so soft."

I'm soft. Nox is hard as hell beneath me. His erection is like a length of steel under my butt cheek.

I want to touch him. I want him to touch me. I want him to move faster, to hit my clit harder, to… to come inside me.

That's what I'm missing. When my pussy is achy and empty even as he's quickened his pace, following the way I'm subtly rocking in his hold… I need something inside of me.

I need Nox.

"Could you…" Regular Amy would never dare to ask, but wanton Amy who might or might not be dealing with something known as mate sickness? She has no shame. "Your finger, Nox. Do you think you could give me something to hold onto? But don't stop what you're doing, okay?"

He might not have any experience—I don't either, really—but he's a quick learner. Once he realized that I squirmed even more every time he bumped my clit, he started paying close attention to the little nub. He's flicking it, stroking it, rubbing it with his thumb while still touching the rest of my pussy with his other fingers.

You know what the best thing about being intimate with a giant shadow demon is, though? The size of their hands. Using his middle finger—still shadowed so his claws are blunt—he finds my entrance and manages to breach it without a hitch.

"Yes," I tell him. I unhook my arm from around his neck, perfectly aware that Nox won't let me fall. Grabbing the arm still wrapped around my waist, I start to lean forward, taking more of his finger inside of me. It's so big and thick, it's almost like what I'd imagine a human dick would be like. "Just like that."

"You're mine," he rumbles. "You always have been. You were born to be my mate and I finally get to have you."

I'm still clinging to his brawny arm, holding on tight, but there's something about the harsh vow in his words that has me second-guessing my earlier "not a perv" assessment. I don't want to stop what I'm doing, but the way he said 'always have been'... I'm sorry. I can't help myself.

This is probably the worst time to ask. His hands are in my pants, his knuckle wedged inside of me, but I have to know.

"When I was a kid," I say, panting slightly as he uses his thumb to strum my clit, almost as if he's unaware that my lust is on hold for the moment, "did you… did you want to mate me then?"

It's Nox's turn to go still. He doesn't pull away from me, though he shifts the angle of his head so that he's staring at my profile. His red eyes flare like a freaking traffic light. Oh, boy. I think I offended him.

Good going, Amy. Why not piss off the massive shadow demon whose claws are inches away from your pussy?

But… wait. I don't think I pissed him off. My first instinct was right. He looks… hurt.

"You were a child," he tells me. "It was my duty as your mate to protect you… to keep you safe so that you could mature. Only then would I look at you and see *my* mate."

He couldn't have answered my question better. Loosening my grip on his arm, I let gravity take over so that I can sink just a little further down on his finger. "And now?" I gasp.

Nox leans in, nuzzling the curve of my neck with his lips. His fangs glide across my skin as he breathes in deep before he rests his chin on my shoulder, looking down at me. "Oh, my sweet, sweet Amy. I *see* you."

That does it. Between the way he crooks his finger inside of me, touching me in a place no one else ever has before except for me, and how he goes back to rubbing my clit, stroking it with a mix of reverence and fierce need, I surrender completely to his hold. To Nox, this is a culmination of a lifetime of fantasies. For me, having my shadow monster finger me to an orgasm *is* my fantasy.

Once I come down from the height of my climax, I collapse against him. I barely notice him shifting me again, gently easing my panties and my jeans back in place, but as suddenly exhausted as I am, no way I don't see the way he dips his fingers into his mouth and rumbles in pleasure.

"Nox…"

I want to tell him that that was the hottest damn thing I've ever seen. The insecure side of me wants to ask if I taste okay, but wanton Amy is slowly giving way to regular Amy. I don't ask, but I don't have to. Nox licks each of his fingers clean with obvious relish, then strokes my hair away from my face.

"Rest," Nox coos, combing his claws through my hair next. I snuggle closer to him, seeking out his warmth—and the continued relief from his touch. "Know you are safe with me, my reason."

My reason?

He's called me his mate. He's called me his Amy. But his reason?

I open my mouth to ask Nox about that, at least. Before I can say a word, it's replaced by a yawn that has my jaw nearly cracking.

Whoa. I guess I didn't realize just how tired I was. Or maybe the orgasm he gave me was enough to relax me for the first time since I caught Connor Hart's attention at the beginning of last year. Either way, I let my mouth close with a soft *click*, then shut my eyes.

I'm out immediately. Like Nox said, I rest, absolutely certain that my monster won't let anything happen to me while he's here.

IT'S NO SURPRISE WHEN I WAKE UP THE NEXT MORNING that I believe that everything that happened last night was a dream. Well, a nightmare if you count what went on with Connor, but seeing Nox again… and the way he pleasured me in the back alley… it seems like another dream.

It wasn't.

My first clue is that it really freaking stinks. My second? That while I don't sleep on silk, my Target sheets get the job done—and they're way softer than the lumpy, sleek, plastic *whatever* that I'm currently laying on top of. Half asleep, I can tell I'm not home, but when last night comes rushing back, I figure out exactly where I am.

I'm sleeping on top of a pile of garbage bags.

My eyes spring open, my heart leaping into my throat. *Shit.* It's bright out. Morning. The street… alley… whatever might have been empty before, but someone's bound to notice a twenty-six-year-old chick laying in the trash—

Oh. Wait. Squinting, I notice a slight haze in front of me. If those are Nox's shadows still hiding me like they did last night, no one will see me.

That doesn't change the fact that I'm curled up in garbage.

Or that I'm alone.

"Nox?" I keep my voice low since I'm not sure if his shadows are soundproof. When I reach inside myself to see if that's something I learned with his essence, I can't find the answer. Better safe than sorry. "Nox, are you still here?"

He said he wouldn't leave me. If those are still his shadows, I want to think he didn't, but Nox never stayed in the human world when it wasn't dark. He called it "the time of shadows", and always slipped away while I was sleeping before it was morning. Now, all these years later, it's morning again, and I don't see him.

At least, I didn't. As soon as I whisper his name, he appears from the farthest end of the street. He was crouched down, melting into the shadows. When he straightens, he shifts from his shadow form to his demon shape as he starts toward me.

I blink, then I gape. This time, though, it's not because he's naked. He's actually not. His bottom half is wrapped in black shadows that seem to drift as he stalks my way. It's like he's woven them into leather pants or something. I don't know. I'm actually kind of distracted by something else.

Nox has chains on him. A dark gold color, there's about a three-foot length of linked chains connected to each of his wrists by a thick manacle. They just about hit the asphalt, dragging as he moves.

Okay… I know they weren't there last night. I'm also pretty sure I saw him wearing chains like those the night those other demons took him away from me.

Where did this set come from?

Better yet, what the hell is he holding in his right hand?

Crawling out of the garbage bags—which is as awkward as it sounds—I climb up from my knees until I'm standing. Good thing I am, because I might've landed back on my ass instead of just stumbling away when I realize what he has.

It's a rat. Dangling from Nox's claws, it's an oversized, dingy grey street rat.

Oh, jeez. Chains or the rat? I'm not sure which one to mention first, and I gesture wildly at him as the big demon puffs out his bare chest proudly.

"I've brought you meat, my mate."

He holds the rat up by the tail so that I can't avoid looking at it. The poor thing is so terrified, it's not even trying to escape. Like a possum, it looks like it's playing dead. If it wasn't for its wild eyes and the few scarce squeaks it lets out, I'd think it *was* dead.

Nox lifts his other hand. Flexing his fingers, he bares his claws. "I thought you would prefer fresh meat. If you're ready to eat, I shall slaughter and skin it for you now."

"No!" Oof. That was loud. I lower my voice. "I mean, no, thank you. I'm not very hungry."

"You haven't eaten since the time of shadows, and I heard your stomach grumbling before while you slept. I'm a hunter, my mate. A provider. I didn't want to go too far from you and there isn't much game nearby, but I found fresh meat."

Right. A rat. "I'd rather you let it go, Nox."

"Are you sure? If you don't want to eat the creature raw, I can start a fire and cook it for you."

I don't know if I'll ever be hungry enough that cooked rat sounds appetizing. Still, I have to remember that Nox is a Sombra demon who hunts his own meals. Just because I'm not used to it doesn't mean I should judge him, especially when he brought the rat back for me.

I shake my head, trying to keep my face from going green. "I'm okay. But if you want to eat it…"

"No. I hunted for my mate, and if she wants me to free the creature, I shall." Bending low, the chains clinking against the ground, he drops the rat a few feet away from me, then nudges it with his toe.

The poor thing flops to its side. Just when I'm sure it died of a rat heart attack or something, it scampers to its feet, then runs off.

Nox wipes his claws along the edge of his shadow pants. "I can always hunt again if you're hungry."

That won't be necessary. My appetite fled at the thought of eating rat, but if it comes back, that bag of candy from last night is probably close by. My purse, too. I'll be fine, and my fridge is full of food from this week's grocery shop. I'm not worried about that.

But I am worried about those chains.

I point. "Those… you weren't wearing them last night." Trust me. With his hands in my pants, his finger inside of me… I would've noticed. "Where did they come from?"

Nox glances down. Holding up his hands, he gazes at the chains as if he's never seen them before.

For a second, I expect him to lie to me. I don't know why. The Nox I remember was honest to a fault —except, I guess, for neglecting to mention that I was his fated mate—but that's not all. A Sombra demon can't lie to his mate. It's something I'm so certain of, I know it's because Nox believes that to his core and it passed over to me with his essence.

So he doesn't lie, but when he answers me, I almost wished he had.

"I've worn these chains since the night Duke

Haures sent his soldiers after me. I broke them to get to you, but I knew it was only a matter of time before they returned. When your yellow sun rose this morning, the cursed chains were back… and now that you have my essence, I can't break them again."

CHAPTER 7
FIRST KISS

AMY

Fourteen years.

Nox has worn those chains for *fourteen* years.

This is what happens when I shut down some of Nox's memories. I'd wondered where he went after those other demons came for him, but I just as quickly shunted it to the side because it didn't matter. He was here with me, and I was too horny to think rationally.

I should've known better. Even as a kid, Nox made me a promise. If I kept him a secret, making sure no one ever knew I had a shadow man for a visitor, he'd never stop coming to see me. And, sure, with adult eyes and ears, I realize how creepy that sounds. Grown men—whether they're human or demon—

probably shouldn't have secrets with little girls. It had seemed so harmless back then, and if I can believe Nox, it was.

Still. I kept my end of the bargain. Not even my mother knew about Nox, though I'm sure she guessed something was up, and we both eventually came to the same conclusion: he was the figment of the imagination of a lonely child. When he was marched out of my room in chains, I was so scared for him—but then it was like he was a fantasy that, at twelve, I was too old to indulge in.

Deep down, though, I wondered. Was it my fault? I kept my secret, but Nox disappeared.

Because, it hits me with a jolt, he was chained and imprisoned. Kept in a dark, dank dungeon cell with a cold bathtub and something like a toilet, a single cot, and no windows, he spent the last fourteen human years as the duke's prisoner for breaking his first law.

Nox crossed into the human world because I called to him with the spell from my Aunt Su's book. Too young to be his mate, he should've gone back until I was older… but he didn't. Worse, I saw him. He told me about Sombra, even going so far as to teach me the language.

Demonkind is supposed to be a secret, just like Nox was. And though I kept that one, too, it didn't matter. Nox broke the law, and he accepted the chains without an argument so that the other demons wouldn't turn their attention on me.

Innocent. The word rises up in my mind, and I know it's how Nox saw me. I was innocent. I didn't deserve to wear a length of cursed chains that would dampen my essence—my soul—and cut me off entirely from my mate.

Well, if you ask me, neither did Nox.

His expression is apologetic, as if he thinks it's his fault that he's trapped in chains again. Not likely. I don't know this Duke guy who runs Sombra, but I blame him. The green-eyed dick of a soldier, too, and the one with purple eyes who lingered in my room after Nox was shoved inside of a portal...

Whoa. *Whoa.* Now that memory? That one's totally mine.

He did something to me. Crouching down, peering under my bed where I was hiding with my fingers shoved against my mouth to keep my cries back, his purple eyes turned white, and then... and then it was all a dream.

Sammael. The name pops into my brain. The duke's mage who conjured the chains that Nox has worn every day since I saw him last.

Fourteen freaking years ago.

And the only reasons he was finally able to get them off were because he sensed how scared I was the moment I locked eyes with Connor, Halloween—or Samhain, as Nox knows it—made the veil between our two very different realms thinner than usual, and he was incredibly motivated to give nearly every bit of essence he had to the cursed chains so that he could snap them long enough to get to me.

Where he then proceeded to sacrifice the last of his essence for me so that I could hide in his shadows.

"Okay. Okay… what does that mean?" I don't want to tap into him again. I just proved it's not as easy as I guess I thought, and I'd rather hear it from him. "You broke out of jail for me? Is that really what happened? Are you serious? Oh my God, Nox!"

I still can't get past this. How did I not know this already? When he gave me his essence, I'm supposed to… I don't know… have gotten, like, a download about Nox. I know everything about him. His age—a number too high for me to really comprehend—and what his life as the hunter in his clan was like. That he's never touched a female before me, and he has no family in Sombra. He was a loner, but after he left me, it's like there's a big gap after the huge shadowy figure with the gleaming green eyes—Glaine… his name rises to the front of my mind this time—*Glaine* came and took him away.

And now it's obvious why. Because he spent the fourteen years we were separated chained and locked in the demon duke's *dungeon*.

Surging forward, I grab the chains, giving them a pitiful tug. "There's gotta be a way to get them off. Maybe not in Sombra, but we have power tools here. Chainsaws, right? Or bolt cutters. We can get them off."

"Not these chains, my mate. If the duke doesn't give the order for the conjurer to break his spell, there's only one way to remove them."

Okay. He would know better than me. "How?"

"When I take you as my mate," Nox says simply. "When we're fully bonded and I have your essence, they won't be able to hold me any longer. Until then, I just have to hope the duke doesn't send his soldiers after me."

"What if he does?"

"I go back to the dungeon."

How… how can he say that so casually? Unless I'm supposed to treat this whole situation the same way.

Fine. I can do that. "We need to be mates for you to be free? Okay. Then let's go."

He eases the chain out of my grip. "I told you, my Amy. Not yet. Not here."

Right. Because I deserve silk. "I have an apartment," I tell him. "It's close by." I think. "We can go there."

"No."

No?

"Why not?"

"It's not safe to leave the shadows yet," is Nox's answer. "We'll stay here."

That's ridiculous. It's early morning, his shadows not as powerful as they were last night, and we both have someone who might be looking for us. He is a fugitive of Sombra, and while I worked hard to convince myself that Connor's probably back in Connecticut by now, I'd have to be a moron to believe that he won't come back to New Jersey. Even if only to figure out what happened in the alley last night when Nox revealed himself to my ex, Connor won't let it go.

He won't let *me* go.

Terror wells inside of me. Only now it's not just my skin I'm worried about anymore. What if those other monsters come for him? What if Connor comes back for me?

What if…

I hug myself. It's a habit I have when everything is suddenly overwhelming and I'm searching for some comfort. I never let anyone but my mom offer it to me before, and I've learned to give it to myself.

Nox notices. Lowering his hands, swing the chains to his side so that they're behind him and mostly out of my sight, he moves closer. "Are you feeling well, my mate?" His gaze locks on the way my arms are wrapped around my middle. "You need to be fed. I should've insisted that you eat the meat."

If I ate rat, I'd probably feel worse. "It's not that."

"Then what is it?"

I shake my head.

Nox gentles his tone. "Without your essence, I don't know all of your thoughts. Your hopes. Your wishes. Your fears. You must share them with me, but I accept if you won't. I'll earn your secrets in time."

Holding out my hand, I say, "I could give it to you now." I don't know how, but Nox can tell me. "My essence, I mean. If that's what you want." And then, sooner or later, we can do the rest of the mating ritual so that, at the very least, the threat hanging over his shiny, black horns is gone.

"What I want is for my mate to prove that she still trusts her male."

Oof. I walked right into that one, didn't I?

Folding my fingers in, forming a fist, I drop it. "I do. It's just… Connor."

"The human male who frightened you."

"Yeah. If it wasn't already clear, he's my ex-boyfriend. Ex-mate—"

The golden chains go from a dark gold to a blinding yellow shade. "You only have one mate, Amelia. Me."

See? I hear 'Amelia', I immediately think I'm in trouble. So though I'm not even a little afraid of Nox, I quickly try my best to diffuse the sudden tension pouring off of my demon. "I know that. Well, now, I do. But Connor, he…" How to explain in a way that he will understand?

Through gritted teeth, he does it for me. "He courted you."

I nod. "Exactly. But, like you said, he's not my

mate. I never really thought of him as one, and when I told him to leave me alone… he didn't."

I don't have to tell him anything else. Just the fact that Connor was caught chasing me—my fear so strong that it called to Nox in a whole other world—is enough to let him know that it was bad.

His eyes blaze, and so do the golden chains stretched between his wrists. His forms wink in and out, from a solid demon to a barely-there shadow before he's back to his red-skinned hulking shape again as he vows, "I'll kill him."

See, that? That's exactly what I was afraid of.

"I can take care of Connor."

"It's my duty to protect you," Nox begins.

I cut him off. "You did last night. You scared him off. If he comes back and you want to do it again, go ahead. Just… don't kill him. For me, okay?"

He huffs. "Always a soft touch, aren't you, my Amy?"

Maybe. Or maybe I'll come to regret it. Doesn't matter. Connor's not the only one making my stomach super uneasy.

"What about you?" I ask. "You broke out of jail for me. If they come back for you, how do I protect you?"

"Amy…"

"Tell me, Nox. Tell me that I don't have to worry about that and I won't. But remember… I have your essence. You can't lie to me."

"I would never," he vows.

"Trust goes both ways," is all I say to that.

"Very well. For you, my mate, I'll tell you."

Something in his tone makes me think that it won't be a brush-off answer like the one I gave him. Figuring I might as well get comfortable, I start to drop down so that I can sit.

I don't get the chance. Before I've even lowered myself into a crouch, Nox scoops me up in his arms. Tucking me close, he settles his big body on the road, nestling me on his lap so that I'm protected from the asphalt.

Then, once he's holding me close, he confirms every single one of my thoughts, suspicions, and the memories that I picked up from his essence when it comes to his time in the dungeon. By the time he's done, my stomach is still tied in knots, and my heart aches for my shadow man.

"I'm so sorry. I wish you hadn't had to go through any of that," I whisper. Especially since, if I hadn't stumbled upon that spell when I was a girl… if I hadn't read the words without understanding what I was doing… Nox wouldn't have had to.

He chucks me under the chin, forcing me to look at him. "I'm not."

"What? Why?"

"An honorable male must prove himself to his mate. I would do anything for you."

"Nox—"

"It's true. Because you are my reason."

"You called me that last night."

"I did. You're my mate, but you're also my reason. My reason to exist. My reason to survive. My reason to hunt, to fight, to *endure*. I do it all for you, and for the chance that, someday, you might return just a fraction of the love I have for you, my mate."

I… I don't know what to say to that. Words fail me, in both Sombran and English. Nothing I could say would ever measure up to his heartfelt confession.

So I don't say a single freaking word. Instead, laying my hands on the edge of his jaw, I take a deep breath and look right into his eyes.

I love him. Probably not the same way he feels for me at this moment, but it's a start. My fond memories of my shadow man, plus the beginning of our mate bond tugging away inside of me… I love him enough for only just getting him back, and it's time I show him how much.

Last night I gave in to my instincts. Wanton Amy went for what she wanted, spurred on by Nox's obvious need and his concern that I was suffering from mate sickness. Curled up in his arms, I wouldn't say no to a repeat of what we did… but that can wait. Because right now? My instincts are telling me to do something a little different.

So I do. I kiss him.

Now, I've kissed guys before. More than a few, though they're all faceless nobodies in the back of my mind as I nip at his lush bottom lip. All human, of course, so when he gets the hint and opens his mouth, the fangs make it a little bit of a challenge. The fact that this is obviously Nox's first kiss doesn't help—but it doesn't hurt, either. In fact, his earnestness to please me makes the first few strokes all the more special.

Like I said before, my shadow monster is a quick learner. His hand goes to my throat, thumb on one side, four fingers on the other, the points of his claws resting on my skin in a careful yet undeniably possessive hold. I melt into him as he takes complete control of the kiss.

As if he can sense that I'm going lightheaded, he finally pulls away. I follow after him, addicted to his taste. After taking another breath, I part my lips, begging him wordlessly to kiss me again.

He does.

It's not fair. My first kiss was messy, sloppy, and unfulfilling. Nox has me keening for more after his. Then again, he's my mate. We're fated. Even if he slobbered, something tells me I'd suddenly find drool sexy as hell.

And, wow, I guess I'm okay with that, too.

He moves away from my mouth, pressing his lips to my nose, my cheek, my forehead. Then, releasing my throat, he cups my chin.

"Stay with me," he whispers roughly, his breath half a pant. "Stay in my shadows."

I'll have to go home eventually—with Nox, hopefully—but for now… I can stay with him a little bit longer.

"Okay."

CHAPTER 8
LEARNING NOX

AMY

I make it until late afternoon before I decide that, despite enjoying this time with Nox, I've hit my freaking limit on being outdoors.

With nothing else to snack on, I broke into the Halloween stash for breakfast. Hours later, I've eaten more candy than I have since probably the last time I trick-or-treated. My teeth feel gritty from all the sugar, I'm thirsty as hell now, and I have to pee.

I already went to the far reaches of Nox's shadows to pop a squat earlier. Between how weird it was peeing out in the open with my jeans waiting for me to the side, knowing that he was watching me closely —and most likely remembering how I let him pet me last night—and also some of it splashing back up at me, hitting my sneakers, I decide that I'd rather take a bladder infection over having to do that again.

On the positive side, the sun's finally started to set. The shadows around us have grown thicker, and as they did, Nox stopped being so vigilant over my every move. From the moment I woke up until now, if I so much as shifted my position, he was alert, and it was starting to get to me.

I guess that's the hunter side of him. He can sit motionless for hours, but the second I move, he does. Unlike how I felt with Connor, I wasn't his prey. He wasn't hunting me—he was *protecting* me. As if he expects that someone will find us in his shadows and snatch me from his grasp, he's watching me with an intensity that I kinda find flattering.

Except for when I had to pee. That was just embarrassing.

We both know it isn't only my ex he's concerned about. So long as those chains are on him, he's marked as a fugitive from Sombra. Sooner or later, we have to face that.

I like to think the sunshine will discourage the other Sombra demons from coming after him, but Nox quickly sets me straight. Not only would his soldiers have the duke's express permission to hop, skip, and jump into the human world, but they'll bring some of Sombra's shadows with them. They won't dare break the duke's first law—the one that says demonkind aren't supposed to mingle with humans—so they'll be completely concealed, regardless of when they finally come for him.

And though he won't admit it to me, I *know* Nox. He's absolutely sure they will.

I try to convince him we should leave. Only… he's not ready to let me out of the protection of his shadows.

Nox isn't human. He doesn't think like we do. He doesn't want Connor finding me. He's desperately trying to stay hidden from the ruler of Sombra and his soldiers. In his mind, that means that we should stay where we're safe. He's proven he can protect this alley and that no one has found us so far. He wants to keep it that way.

Which is probably why, after I suggest that maybe we don't have to stay hiding among the trash bags, his whole attitude seems to change.

The vigilance from before has turned to something else. Something more… primal, I'd say.

He starts to prowl. Instead of hovering over me, watching me closely, he puts some distance between us as he slips along the edges of the alley. He stays to the shadows. His eyes are never off me for more than a few seconds. There's a charge in the air, though, and when he thinks he's too far for me to notice, he reaches down to his crotch and gives himself a quick stroke.

He's still hard. Throughout today, he's gone from completely shadow to fully demonic so many times, I lost track. At some point, he stopped conjuring his shadow coverings when he was in his solid form so it was pretty obvious that his hard-on hasn't gone down yet.

I shouldn't be staring. Like last night, I should be a decent chick and keep my eyes above his chest. When he was sitting next to me, I could. When he's prowling like that, reminding me just how inhuman he is? I can't stop myself from ogling my demon.

Just like I can't stop myself from finally giving in to my lust.

If he's not going to take care of his little—er, big—problem, why can't I?

"Hey, Nox?"

His head swivels toward me. He'd been just about to pass me, giving me another peek at his tight ass, but he stops in the middle of his step. "Yes, my mate?"

"Can you come here?"

He doesn't hesitate and, holy hell, is he fast. Before I know it, he's crouched right in front of me.

Perfect. I go from sitting on my ass to rising up to my knees in front of him. With his height, I'm at just the right angle to take his bobbing, erect cock between both of my hands.

He sucks in a breath. "Amy…"

"Is this… is this okay? Can I—"

His voice has gone throaty and deep as he tells

me, "I'm yours. I've always been yours. That includes every part of me. Whatever you want to do to me… *please*."

It takes both hands to take him from root to tip. He shudders with the first stroke. I shudder with the second. Just like I thought, his dick is hot. It's heavy. It's *hard*. But it's also soft enough to entice me to run my fingers along the thickest vein. Blood rushing to his erection, it's almost freaking pulsing.

I squeeze. Nox groans. I like the sound so much, I do it again.

That's when he places his hand over mine, a clear signal if I've ever seen one.

"Is everything okay?" I freeze because, up until now, I thought it was. "Do you want me to stop?"

"I want you to answer a question." Instead of pulling away from me, he lowers his crouch so that he's kneeling in front of me. "Is this the mate sickness again?"

I don't think so. Honestly, I don't think it was last night, either.

If I'm his mate, then he's mine. This is just me finally exploring my sexuality for the first time in my life with someone I trust—and who I'm undeniably attracted to.

Not only that, but Nox has done so much for me. As a kid, he helped me get through one of the roughest times of my life. Now… I don't want to mate him to make us even, or because having my own personal shadow monster will stop Connor from coming back. I want to be his mate because it… it feels right. It's almost like I've known all along I was waiting for him to return to me.

This is Nox. He's mine, and if I have to make the first moves to show him that I haven't been afraid of the bogeyman since I was nine—and that I've been fantasizing about fucking a demon… my demon… since I was nineteen—then I will.

"No," I tell him honestly. "This is just me wanting to get to know you even better… if that's okay."

"I told you, my mate. I'm yours. If it pleases you to touch me, do it. Learn your male."

I will.

I start out slow. Instead of tightening my grip, I release one of my hands. While still trailing my fingers down his length, I reach beneath him with the other. I find his balls, smiling when Nox grunts as I play with them. I notice then that he's finally broken his seal. A bead of pre-come is glistening on the crown of his dick. I've gotta admit, it's a relief to see that it's a recognizable color. I don't know what I would've done if his jizz was black like shadows or something, but, thank God, I don't have to deal with that.

Nox slowly starts to rock his lower body. He's moving in time to my leisurely stroke, and though he doesn't make any instructions—something Connor did constantly—I get the hint. I grab him with both hands again, squeezing him tight as I pick up the pace.

Glancing up, I see that he's gritting his teeth, fangs digging past his bottom lip. It makes the edge of his jaw go impossibly sharp, his profile both masculine and stunning. So what if he's a demon? He's my demon, and I've never been so attracted to anyone before in my life.

He's close. Super close. Actually closer than I guessed because, after only a couple of strokes, he begins to buck into my fists.

As he comes, he grunts out my name, and my smile only widens.

Too bad the high from Nox's release doesn't last.

Reality is setting in. And reality says that I haven't been home in almost twenty-four hours.

Whether anyone else notices that I'm gone, it doesn't matter. My mom will. Since I moved into my own place, I've checked in with her every night after dinner. She didn't ask me to, but it was something I did when I dormed at college. Once I was living a state away from her, I fell back into the old habit.

Considering she's the only one—apart from Laura—who knows that I left because I was trying to avoid Connor, those nightly check-ins assure her that I'm safe. I called her last night before Francesca knocked on my door, but she hasn't heard from me since.

I thought about calling her earlier. Stowed at the bottom of my purse, I have the cheap pay-as-you-go phone that I keep topped up with minutes for emergencies like this. Too bad I haven't charged it in a couple of days and it was completely dead when I reached for it.

After Nox finished, I used the sleeve of my hoodie to wipe up the come that spattered on my hand and the thighs of my jeans. Once he started bucking in my hand, I tried to angle him before he got it all over me, but not only did I underestimate how quick he was to go off, but demon come? It's thick and white and ropy like a human guy's, only there's way more of it.

Even more interesting, Sombra demons aren't a "one and done". With Connor, he would take a handjob and be satisfied, rolling over to spoon behind me while I tried to scoot away from him in case he got any ideas. My mate? After his orgasm, his cock is still as hard as it was before I first took him in my hand.

I wasn't sure what I was supposed to do after I noticed, but Nox made the decision easy. While murmuring softly under his breath in Sombran, he began to conjure another set of shadows that basically acted like his clothing. I was glad to see that, just because he was in chains, he had control of his abilities. I had worried before when I noticed that he kept going from his solid form to fully shadows, but the chains didn't seem to do anything other than keep him from spreading his arms open wide. That's okay, though. There's enough of a length that he can loop the chains around me in order to hold my body close to his.

Conjuring the shadow pants is a sure sign that he doesn't expect me to do anything more than I have before I can even figure out what I *would* do.

I don't regret what just happened between us. Maybe now that I'm covered in dirt from the alley, things I don't want to think about from the trash bags, and now Nox's jizz… if I don't get to use a bathroom and soon, I might lose it. But I don't regret it at all. I was happy to prove to Nox that I'm as attracted to him as he is to me, no mate sickness involved.

Though maybe I shouldn't have immediately told him after he finished that I thought it was time I finally use the dark shadows to go back home…

He frowns. "You didn't pleasure me just to get your whim, did you? Because I'll give you anything, my mate. Anything you want… you just have to ask. Tell me you want it and it's yours. Don't feel like you must control your mate through his cock."

Is that what he thinks?

"I don't. Look, you have to admit that this is new to both of us. And I understand why you wanted to keep me close last night, but… the human world is different, Nox. I've never slept outside before, and I'd really rather not do that again. Do you understand?"

"I do."

"Good."

"You want to leave me. Was this"—he gestures down to his covered cock—"your way of telling me goodbye?"

Oh. So he doesn't understand even a little.

Overprotective and snarling when he faces a threat, gentle when he touches me intimately, and insecure when he feels a hint of rejection… I'm learning more and more about my shadow man.

I snag two of his fingers, the most I can wrap my hand around without struggling. "No. You got it wrong… I want you to come with me. That's what I meant. We go together."

That mollifies my monster a little. Still, Nox shows his stubborn side as he insists, "I can keep you safe in my shadows. I've marked this territory as mine. We don't have to leave it."

"But you can also use your shadows inside, right? Like, if you want to keep me wrapped up inside of them while we're in my apartment… that's possible, isn't it?"

"Apartment," he echoes. "Your quarters? Your den?"

If that's what he wants to call it. "My home, yes. I have food there, Nox. A toilet." A *bed*. "Locks, too. They might not be enough to keep other demons out, but at least I know that Connor won't be able to get in."

That does it. Whether Nox holds true to his vow that all I had to do is ask him for what I want, or if he's keen on the idea that my ex-mate won't be able to get to me… it doesn't matter. He nods.

Between one blink and the next, the shadows that covered most of the alleyway have condensed. They surround Nox, turning him into an amorphous shape with only the dimmest red eyes. He's hidden—and I'm freed.

Huh. I don't know how I feel about that. On the one hand, I get it. It's essential that no other human catches a single glimpse of Nox; wrapped up in his shadows the way he is, only I'm able to and that's because I have his essence. I'm human. A smelly mess of a human, sure, but no one on the streets will look twice. Actually, they might not even look once if they think there's something mentally off with me.

Does that stop me from being just a little dejected now that I don't feel the safety net of Nox's shadows? Nope. But I'm a big girl so I just swoop down, grabbing the plastic bag with the Halloween candy in it first, then my purse.

"I'm ready when you are," I tell him.

His voice is a whisper. "Lead the way."

I'm gonna try. Considering I'm not so sure where Connor chased me off to last night, it might take a couple of tries before I lead us to my apartment building. I keep that to myself. I'm the one who told him that I wanted off the street. If I left it up to him, no doubt we'd spend another night in the garbage.

No, thanks.

For once, it looks like luck is on my side. Not only is the main road our alley is tucked off of as empty as it was last night, but that gives me the chance to backtrack my steps without a whistling stalker hustling behind me. Without panic blinding me to most of my surroundings, it isn't too difficult to stumble upon a street I recognize as one a couple of blocks away from my apartment.

Even better, there's a payphone on the corner.

In some ways, Sombra is as technologically advanced as the human world. That surprised me. With Nox a hunter, I just assumed it was a hunter-gatherer-type of society. And while that's true, and they don't have things like electricity or the internet, they have magic. They've got toilets, too, which is a win in my book, but it's not as backward as my human-centric ego led me to believe.

They don't have phones, though. He seemed both amused and a little wary when I pulled mine out of my purse. I think he understood it better when I explained it was a way to contact my family; or my kin, as he referred to my mother. Though Sombra demons are basically immortal, if you leave your clan, you lose your birth family. That's what Nox did. He joined the clan in Nuit, so he has no family of his own that he claims. Even so, it's obvious how important my mother is to me.

I pause. Then, keeping my voice low, I say, "See that boxy-looking thing over there?"

He brushes against the back of his neck with his shadows. I take that as a 'yes'.

"It's a phone. I don't have a landline set up in my apartment yet, and my cell phone will need time to recharge. Do you mind if I call my mom real quick?"

Another stroke. This one I interpret as a 'no'.

"Thank you, baby," I murmur. It just slips out. I mean, Nox is freaking huge. Calling him 'baby' is like picking out the bulkiest guy in a biker club and nick-naming him 'Tiny'... but… I don't know. It sounded right in the moment.

"My reason." His voice as soft as a breeze, I know then that he doesn't mind. In fact, through the pulse of pure pleasure blooming inside of my chest, I'm pretty sure he likes it.

That seals it. My shadow monster is my 'baby' now.

Scurrying over to the payphone, I dig around the bottom of my purse. I scowl when the back of my hand hits the worthless phone in there, though my expression becomes one of triumph when I pull out a handful of change.

Local calls are fifty cents. When I was younger, before everyone and their brother had a cell phone, we used to dial collect, spit out the message for our parents—*movie'sdone,youcancomegetmenow*—then hang up before anyone had to pay. Long distance is at least a dollar now, but I'm freaking twenty-six. If my mom gets a collect call from me, she'll be heading toward New Jersey in a heartbeat to make sure I'm doing all right on my own.

As I'm feeding quarters into the slot, dialing the home number we've had since I was nine, I sense Nox drifting past me. My finger hovers over the last number, watching what he's doing.

This street is one of the busier ones in my new neighborhood. Not as hectic as the one that has the convenience store on the corner, but it's not empty. Up ahead, there's a group of four guys about my age hanging out, sharing a smoke. There's a video store that's still open, neons bathing the sidewalk with a reddish glow.

There's parallel parking, too. Not all the spots are taken, but there's a car about six feet away from the payphone. The driver is sitting in the front seat, the engine humming as he busies himself doing who knows what. Music seeps out through the closed windows.

Squinting, I see that Nox is drifting toward it. I can sense the curiosity wafting off of him.

Makes sense. He admitted that he's never been outside in the human world before. Without anyone passing by our alley, he wouldn't have seen a car until now. At least, not one that was on. The heat of the exhaust is sending cloudy-looking puffs into the chilly night air, and that's where Nox stops. He seems fascinated.

Good. I jab my thumb on the 'eight' button, then lift the receiver to my face. He can look at the car while I make my call.

CHAPTER 9
ACCIDENT

AMY

I thought my mom would be waiting by the phone. This is later than usual for me, but after the phone rings seven times, the call is just clicking over to the answering machine when it happens.

Later on, I still won't be able to explain exactly *what* happened. Between how the reddish glow from the neons left the street washed out, how dark Nox's shadows were, tucked against the side of the car, and just how distracted I was… I don't even know I would've noticed at all if it wasn't for how the car's reverse lights went on and, suddenly, I saw that there was a fully formed demon Nox standing there.

My first instinct is to freak out that someone will see him. The four guys on the corner, or the driver looking in his rearview… a mortal will see him and he'll be in so much trouble.

And then… and then he's gone. I don't mean he shifted back to his shadow form, either. I mean *gone*, like something knocked him down.

The chains. The goddamn chains. Somehow, when he went from shadow to solid, the chains passed through the wheel on the car, then got tangled up in it. As the driver reversed, then pulled out of his spot, the chains took Nox with him.

It takes a second for me to realize what's going on. By then my shadow monster has been dragged under the car. I can't tell if he was run over or what, but I drop the payphone and make a break for the car just as the idiot driver realizes that there's something big being dragged beneath his car.

I swallow my scream, hoping like hell that Nox is okay, and that no one else saw him before he went down. I know he'll be okay. Demons… they can't die. They're immortal. Sure, that didn't tickle—and I know that for a fact since my arms are freaking on fire with the burn of road rash right about now—but he'll heal. He has to.

If the stupid duke has more proof that multiple humans saw him… demons don't die. But they can be executed.

No fucking way.

Just as I reach the car, prepared to throw myself under it to get to Nox, the driver finally figures out something is wrong and stops. I don't even think. I just react. Tossing my purse beneath the nearest tire, I shriek right as the driver pops his door and hurries out of his car.

"My purse," I yell. "You drove off with my purse!"

Anyone with a brain would realize that a regular-sized woman's purse would never make the kind of thump and thud that Nox's brawny demon body would. Plus, I was on the phone. I wasn't anywhere near his car when he pulled out of his spot, and even if I was, how did he drive off with my purse? It doesn't make sense.

Luckily, the driver is either a huge freaking idiot—or he just wants to make sure his car is okay.

"What? Are you sure? It felt like I hit something fucking huge."

Yeah. My mate.

Throwing myself to my hands and knees, I reach under the car. I grab my purse to back up my story, but my attention is entirely on Nox.

He's turned to mist. The softest form of shadow that he can be. I ghost my fingers through the haze, making sure he knows that I'm here with him and that it's time to go, then babble a nonsense apology to the driver as I hop back to my feet, showing off my battered purse.

Do I know what I'm saying? Nope. I need to get out of here before he realizes that he might've seen something that he shouldn't have—or that there was no conceivable way that he snagged my purse or it thumped enough like Nox's body did as it dragged down the street.

Through the fledgling mate bond we have, I can still feel the echoes of his pain. I'm pretty sure he'll deny it, but that had to have hurt.

I also have no clue what happened. He told me that, so long as he was shadow, the only mortal who could sense him was me because of our mate bond. That's true while he's faded from the inky black shadow shape I'm so used to, but what about the solid, red-skinned demon? I can't say it's a good thing that his chains got snagged and he went down before anyone else saw him. It's not. Why did he change shapes, though? Is he looking for a reason to go back to Sombra?

Or was that out of his control?

Right now, it doesn't matter. I need to get Nox off of the street. We can figure this out in the safety of my apartment.

So, clutching my purse, I wave at the bewildered driver, then make my escape, only pausing for a second to check that Nox's shadows have joined mine. Once I see that he's there, if almost completely faded, I start to jog.

And if I'm reminded of last night? I shove that thought out of my head as fast as humanly possible. I have to make sure that my demon is okay.

I just got him back. I'm not about to lose him again.

NOX

My shadows are failing me.

For more than twelve centuries, I've been able to control shifting without even a conscious thought. If I needed to be shadow, I was shadow. If my demonic form was needed, I went solid. Easy as that.

Until I returned to the human world.

I wanted to believe the sunlight from earlier weakened me, and while that's true, it was more than that. Even before the time of shadows was done, I'd noticed that I was shifting for no reason at all. I might not have had to give my body the command, but I was in control of what shape I was in. Not any longer.

Is it the chains? While they mark me as one of the duke's prisoners, their main purpose is to feed on my essence to weaken me. But I no longer have essence of my own. I gave the last of it to my Amy.

But, before I did, I fed nearly all of it into the chains to break them. Is that where I made my mistake? By sacrificing so much, did I make it so that I'm a danger to my mate?

I'd never hurt her. She must know that. I believe she does, despite how much she wanted to escape the territory I provided for us both. I have to remember that she is no demoness from a realm like mine. She's human. Delicate. Breakable.

And I want to rut her like a wild beast.

My need has only grown since she laid her dainty little hands on my throbbing cock. If I'm being honest with myself, if I wanted to keep her stolen to my shadows, I would've had my way with that. I would've insisted, and even if Amy argued, I'm her male. I'll do what I must to protect her, even from herself.

But she mentioned her quarters. For a terrible moment, I thought she was trying to leave me. No. My precious mate was inviting me to follow her home, where she would feel safe and I would learn more about the female she's grown into.

I also hoped to be able to pleasure her again. It was the highlight of my long life when she allowed me to stroke her cunt. After the small taste of her I got, licking my claws clean, I hunger to bury my face between her thighs. She told me after she took my cock in her hands that it wasn't the mate sickness leading her to want to touch me. She did so of her own accord, just like she allowed me to touch her.

I want to do more. I want to mate my human, to make her mine so that no one on this plane or any other can come between us. Not the human male I would hunt if she allowed me to, or Duke Haures and his soldiers.

Would she allow me to pleasure her again this night? I'd hoped so. Even if she wasn't ready to bond herself to me, now that our mate bond is fully in place, I have until the gold moon in Sombra rises before I have to either willingly walk back into my cell again or release Amy from it.

According to my mate, I spent fourteen human years already imprisoned. To keep my tie to her, I'd keep my chains. I'd return to my cell. Anything for Amy.

But can I walk away?

I should. After what just happened, I know I should.

My shadows failed, and I ended up under the human vehicle I'd been examining, making sure it was no threat to my Amy while she used the communication device to contact her kin. I was more surprised at my loss of control than pained by the way the smooth yet also quite pebbly street tore up my back and upper arms as I was dragged before I slipped into my shadow form again.

Amy felt that. She experienced phantom pains from my own injury, but she proved to me that she is still the smart female I've long adored. She saved me. Drawing the attention of the human, she came up with a story to satisfy his curiosity without him ever learning that he was in the presence of a hunter from Sombra. Then, after making sure I was with her, she brought me to her home.

I didn't think I could feel any worse—and then I see the structure that Amy calls hers. It seems to stretch miles high into the sky, so much more impressive than the home I began building for our mating once she summoned me to her side.

"This is all yours?" I rumble, trying to hide how dismayed I am. If this is what my Amy is used to, a humble hunter can never provide her the same.

How will I get her to follow me to Sombra when the human world has this to offer her?

Amy glances up. She was digging around her bag again—her purse—searching for something else. I don't know what else she can have in there. I've seen her phone. Coin. Something she called 'chapstick' that made her lips taste delicious when I initiated another kiss.

Ah. She pulls out something that jangles, then shakes her head. "I'm on the sixth floor. I've got 6C, that's all."

I'm not sure what that means until she leads me into a small room that seems to move though we're not going anywhere. She checks to see that I'm still shadow—I went solid for a few seconds while she was rummaging through the white tote she kept her candies in, but I shifted back before she saw—then gestures for me to follow her into a hall that looks exactly the same as the one we were in when she led me into the small room.

A row of doors is in front of us. Amy picks one, then uses the metallic stick in her hand to open it. She ushers me in, tossing her candies tote and her purse onto the first piece of furniture she sees.

That, too, is finer than anything that once was in my home, I notice.

As soon as her hands are empty, she motions for me to stay put. Though I'm not sure where she thinks I would go otherwise, I jerk my head in a nod.

She bolts from the room.

I'm curious. Being curious is better than scowling, I decide. I don't want to leave the spot Amy told me to wait in, so I look around while keeping my feet planted on her floor. It's soft, like my mate. Almost fuzzy between my toes.

With a frown, I look down. Oh. I shifted from shadow to demon again so that's why I'm completely tangible.

Minutes pass. I hear a strange sound, then a yelp from Amy. She calls out, "I'm fine, be right out," so I stop rushing toward her, hurrying back to the same spot I'd been standing on. She told me to stay there. I will do as she requested.

It seems like an eternity, though I know it's been no time at all before she comes back. She's taken off one layer of her coverings, swapping the other for a top that allows me to see the outline of her full breasts. Same with her bottoms. The rough, dark material that enclosed her legs has been traded for a skimpy covering barely larger than her… what did she call them? Ah. Her panties.

The foul odor that followed us from the alley is gone. All that's left is Amy's sweet scent, beckoning me to her.

I swallow roughly. She hasn't told me I could move yet.

She makes a small sound of surprise in the back of her throat when she sees that I'm a demon again. Then, nodding to herself, she circles me, moving to stand at my back.

I stay standing in one place.

"Huh. Look at that."

I can not. "Amy?"

Her hand lands on the back of my upper arm. "You're healed," she says. "From the accident with that stupid car… you're okay."

Of course I am. I'm a Sombra demon male. As soon as I turned to shadow, the injuries to my demonic form were healed instantly.

She seems so surprised. With my essence inside of her, she should know that. Then again, it will take some time for her to be able to wade through twelve centuries of my thoughts, memories, and experiences. Like how she didn't know of my time in the dungeon until she pressed me to confess it to her, there are details I take for granted that she'll learn in time.

As she learned me…

Her touch is like a whisper against my skin. So soft. So gentle. I want to preen, leaning against her palm so that I feel her everywhere.

I think back to earlier this afternoon. It's impossible not to. How she wrapped her fingers around my cock, stroking me to completion for the first time since I put on the chains.

I'm still wearing them. They've been part of me for so long, I barely notice them. That would explain my… accident, though, wouldn't it? I neglected the chains and, because of that, I ended up being attacked by the vehicle. The car.

Some protector I am. My wee human mate had to save me.

I'm proud of her. Furious at myself, but proud of my Amy. And if the price I had to pay to get her hands on me again was ripping my flesh open on the human ground, I'd do it again, so long as I didn't upset my mate.

I did before. The fear scent came back when she chased after me, and it lingered during the trip to her home. It's gone now, thank the gods.

Taking a deep breath, I let her sweet scent settle around me for a moment before a new note starts winding its way into it.

Lust. My Amy smells like lust.

And it's *delicious*.

"Amy?" I ask again.

She moves in front of me, a determined look on her lovely face. My heart skips a beat, breath getting caught in my lungs when she tilts her head up, meeting my gaze without any hesitation.

She doesn't look away, even as she reaches down, grabbing the length of chain.

"You told me that there's a couple of full-proof ways to get rid of this sucker, right?"

"I… yes. Two that I know of."

"I only care about one." Wrapping the chain around her tiny fist, she tugs. Following her lead, I stumble forward, bracing my hands on her slender shoulders. "Okay. Let's do it. Let's mate."

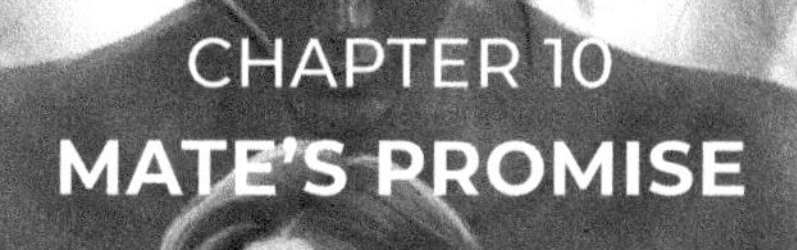

CHAPTER 10
MATE'S PROMISE

AMY

If it wasn't for the fact that he's making it after I flat-out proposition him for sex, the expression on Nox's strikingly handsome face would be hysterical.

Since he did on the heels of me offering to sleep with him, it's not funny. Not funny at all.

"Forget it." I wave my hand. "It was just an idea."

"Amy…" He bows his head, then licks his bottom lip. "I want to. I want you. But only if you understand… I'll expect the mate's promise. I'll demand your essence. When I mate you, I'll make you my mate. You'll be mine forever."

Forever… that means something to a Sombra demon. Almost completely immortal, if I become his mate, I'll live just as long as he will—with him. There are no take-backs. No divorces. No changing your mind.

I reach down and grab the hem of my t-shirt, then yank it over my head.

Good.

"That's what I was hoping for, baby. Way I see it, this kills two birds with one stone. I get my mate, and you get rid of your chains. We can't lose."

When Nox doesn't answer me, I notice that he's staring at my boobs. Like, the *lights are on but nobody's home* kind of staring.

I swallow my giggle. If I had any doubts that he wanted me as badly as I want him, they're gone in an instant.

"Nox, baby? You listening to me?"

Maybe he is. Probably is. He's also transfixed by the sight of my boobs in my bra.

Only… he doesn't seem to be a fan of the material hiding my nipples from him. Just like he didn't know what panties are, he seems unfamiliar with a bra. So my fierce male does what he's done his whole long life when confronted with something he doesn't understand.

He lashes out with his claws. He doesn't get my skin at all, but the points tear through the material as though it were tissue instead of an expensive piece of underwear.

"Nox!"

He doesn't understand money. In Sombra, they

barter. Maybe in their capital city they use coin, but not in Nuit. He'd have no idea if I told him that he just sliced a forty-dollar bra in two pieces, and since I'd rather start the mating process than explain how overpriced Victoria's Secret bras are, I let it go.

I do, however, yank off my sleep shorts and my panties before he can get his claws anywhere near them.

As soon as I'm completely naked, I wait for him to dissolve the shadow coverings around his legs before I hop onto the bed. For my first time, I figure going missionary is the best way to start, so I prop myself up on the pillow and pat the bed so that Nox knows to join me.

When he climbs up, one thigh on the edge of the bed and his erection pointing like an arrow at me, I admit I have a little bit of reservation. It's freaking huge, but I'll make this work.

I have to.

Because this? This is happening. I'm not some shy virgin because of, like, purity culture or because someone told me all good girls wait. That's crap. I'm a virgin because the idea of physically sleeping with a guy had my skin crawling for as far back as I could remember.

Now I know why. I was fated to mate a demon male and not a human man, and as soon as he climbs on top of me, moving gingerly as if desperate not to use his size against me, I know it's about to happen.

Grabbing his dick in one of his huge hands, he moves it toward the entrance to my pussy. And then… it doesn't happen at all.

I can feel the blunt head nudging me. I'm so wet, he slips right off. Isn't he supposed to, like, get in position and shove? That's what I expected would happen. Even though he's so big, fate wouldn't make me his mate if we didn't fit.

Right?

Shifting my ass on the sheet, I try to see if I can help him find the hole. It's not working. I lean up on my elbows, watching him look helplessly at me.

Great. Two virgins fumbling around, neither one of us having any real idea what we're doing.

It's supposed to be instinctive. At least, that's what Nox believes. He has a dick. I've got a pussy. Stick it in, bounce around, and we'll be mates. The rest can work itself out. The fucking part… that's not optional.

So what's going on?

As if he can sense my frustration, Nox pulls back. The head of his cock is shiny from all of my juices. I'm definitely aroused enough to be able to at least get the head inside of me—right?

"What is it?" he asks me. "Am I doing something wrong?"

"No. It's just…"

How do I explain? That it's not him. It's me.

I'm willing. More than willing. But then I keep thinking of just how big he is, how small I am in comparison, and the mental image of a battering ram keeps popping into my brain at the worst moment.

I'm not only tight. I'm freaking tense.

I need to relax. I need Nox to take me out of my head for a moment.

"Let's get back to that," I suggest. "Why don't you kiss me first?"

"Oh, my reason," he says in a husky voice. "I was hoping you'd give me that honor."

Huh? Why did he say it like that? We've already kissed. A couple of times already, actually. Once I showed him how to do it, my quick learner over here was eager to practice again and again. So… honor?

I understand what he means a second later.

One moment I'm flat on my back. The next? I'm sitting on his face.

Nox doesn't want to kiss my mouth. He wants to kiss my pussy, and he proves it by dragging the flat of his long, thick tongue all the way up my slit.

I squeal when he hits my clit.

Taking that as a sign that he did something right, Nox sucks it into the heat of his mouth. He nuzzles the top of my pussy as he does before turning his attention to one of my labia. He nibbles before dipping his chin and beginning to feast on my whole freaking vagina.

He doesn't stop. The more of my taste he gets, the more ravenous my monster becomes.

Right when I begin to worry about whether he's getting enough oxygen down there, I try to lift myself.

Using his blunted claws, he digs into my thighs just enough to make it clear: he doesn't want me going anywhere.

"Nox!" I'm a bigger than average-sized gal, both in height and weight, though standing next to Nox makes me feel delicate and petite. "I'm gonna suffocate you!"

His voice is muffled—obviously—but I can still make out the chuckle that tickles my pussy before he says, "You can not, my wee mortal. But if so, I would go to the gods the happiest male to ever exist. Now, grasp my horns. I'm going to kiss my female and I don't want you going anywhere."

Well. If that's how he really feels.

I take his horns in my hands, riding him as he works magic with his tongue. I figure he'll tell me if he changes his mind so I decide to let wanton Amy out for a little bit. It's probably for the best since, within a few minutes, I'm squeezing the sides of his head between my thighs as I'm about to come on his face.

And then he dips the point of his tongue inside of my pussy and I do.

As the orgasm hits me, I try to pull away again. Nox isn't having that. Fucking me with his tongue, it's a promise of what he'll do to me once I'm ready to let his dick have a turn.

It isn't long before I am.

"Nox... *please...*"

He hears something in my mewling voice. Withdrawing his tongue, he lifts me up and off of him, looping the golden chains behind me so that they're still not a barrier between us. After he sets me back on the bed, he moves so that he's kneeling between my legs. His hand is on his cock, pumping it once, then one more time.

I thought it was because he was checking to see if it was still hard. That's... that's not what he's doing. When Nox moves his hand the second time, I see that he's turned his whole dick into a shadow of what it was. Inky black and noticeably smaller than before—if still pretty huge—he angles it toward me.

I have to ask. "What... what happened to you?"

"It occurred to me as I mated you with my tongue. I must remember that you're so much smaller than I am. In this form, I will also dwarf you. But if I can turn my claws to shadow to keep from scratching you, why couldn't I do the same to my cock? I can feed it into your cunt, then mate you. It's still me. In either form, I am your male. It'll be easier for you to take me, though. Unless you'd rather not."

After what he just did to me? I'm so empty and achy and hot, I think he was right. I'm ready to take that monstrous cock of his.

However, if he thinks this might be easier... I'm not going to complain.

"I want you inside me," I tell him honestly. "Whatever way I can get you."

"You have my heart. You have my soul. And, now," he grips his dick by the base, moving so that he's in between my legs while I lay flat on my back again, "you have my cock."

With his cock positioned at the entrance to my pussy, Nox leans down. I expect him to start pushing again. He doesn't.

Instead, his breath fans my overheated face as he says, "I took my kiss. Now I'll give you yours."

Oh my God. I taste myself as Nox presses his lips against mine. I've never done anything so erotic before, but I'd be lying if I said it didn't turn me on even more.

Which, I think, was part of his plot. Because, even as he strokes my tongue with his, he begins to work himself inside of me.

I'm soaking wet. The orgasm he gave me relaxed me enough after the way he fucked me with his tongue. This time there's no resistance at all when he exchanges his tongue for his cock. Whether it's because he kept his dick in his shadow form while being hot and heavy and red everywhere else, or because I'm so far gone that I'm not even thinking about how big he is… it doesn't matter. There's a pinch, a moment of shocking fullness, and a pause as Nox situates himself while also giving me time to adjust to having inside of me.

He breaks the kiss, nuzzling my cheek with his chin. "Ready, my mate?"

I nod. "I'm ready to be your mate, baby."

I watch the motion in his throat as he swallows roughly. Slowly, he pulls back, dragging his cock through my pussy. The sensation sends shivers down my spine. I groan.

He grunts.

"Give me your essence, my reason. Give me everything you have."

I don't know how, but I'll try.

I hook both of my arms around his neck, sliding across my sheets as he slowly rocks into me. Too consumed by the absolute pleasure of being stuffed full of my demon, his shadows reaching to every part inside of me, there's no pain. I'm sure there'll be some tomorrow. But that's tomorrow. Tonight I'm just going along for the ride.

The faster he goes, the more I move with him. He's careful to keep the chains over my head instead of looped behind my back like before. The bed squeaks, the chains rattling, but that's nothing compared to his feverish grunts and my throaty moans as we mate.

Eventually Nox notices that the force of his thrusts is causing my whole body to move with the motion. Again, he lowers his head, putting his horns within my grasp. Letting go of his neck, I take one in each hand and… oh. *Oh.* Not only does this put me in a much better position to mate my monster, but it changes the angle of his thrusts just enough to have my eyes nearly rolling in the back of my head.

It does something to Nox, too. The slow strokes from the beginning have quickened into a frantic pace, almost as if we're in a race to see who finishes first.

Me. It's totally going to be me.

I'm panting. My legs are shaking beneath him, the chains rattling behind my head with another of his powerful thrusts. His eyes are brighter than I've ever seen them. As he locks gazes with me, their shine almost hypnotizes me.

I don't blink, though. I can't. Something momentous is happening between us and I'm not about to miss a minute of it.

I take my hands off his horns. I hold out one. He takes it, wrapping his mitt-sized hand around mine. He's strong enough to keep himself from crushing me with only one arm, and I need this. He has his connection. I have mine.

And, once we're done, we'll have another. One that's ours.

I can't freaking wait.

"My soul will be yours," Nox promises solemnly.

"My soul will be yours," I repeat back.

I'm not really sure why. It seems like something I was supposed to do, so I did.

Rumbling in pleasure, he bends his braced arm

just enough that our bodies are slicking together as he rocks into me. He's not even pulling out partway and thrusting back in anymore, and I don't think it's because I'm making him hold my hand or that his chains are constraining. As if he can't bear to break the connection at all, he's shortened his motion while also moving even faster.

We're still racing—and making our mate's promise.

"My heart is in your hands."

I swallow my moan. "My heart is in your hands."

His voice drops. Sweat drips from his brow, landing on the height of my cheek. "Our lives will be forever intertwined."

"Our lives will be forever intertwined," I swear.

"I give myself to you." He pauses, bucking into me, then vows, "I give you everything."

"I do," I tell him. "I give myself to you. I give you everything, Nox."

"I accept it," he grunts, thrusting again until he's seated fully inside of me. Wiggling his arms on both sides, he jerks the chains so that they're nestled beneath my neck. "And now I give you my seed."

Something about the way he says that in his deep voice makes it sound so filthy. I mean, I didn't expect Nox to shout out he was coming or tell me he's ready to bust a nut or anything, but his seed?

That's so fucking hot. And, considering his body temperature is so much higher than mine, I mean that literally. I can actually *feel* the warmth as he throws his horns back and roars his release.

I already knew he shot more than a human male. What I wasn't prepared for was how long he would continue to keep himself buried deep inside of me so that he could empty his entire sac.

By the time he's done and he finally pulls out, I can't freaking move. I'm completely spent. Pleasured within an inch of my life, and feeling whole for the first time since those soldiers stole my shadow man from me, but also absolutely exhausted.

Leaning over me, Nox kisses me again. I have just enough energy to return it. I vaguely notice that he's cupped my neck, lifting me off of the bed for a second before he sets me back down.

He's freed me from his chains. They rattle as he pulls them closer to him as he rises up off of the bed and moves toward the foot of it.

He knows where the bathroom is. I pointed it out in case he needed to use it. Figuring he's heading there, I lay back down. Hopefully he can figure it out on his own.

Only he doesn't head toward the bathroom. Instead, he crouches low, then grabs me by my ankles. I go shooting across the rumpled sheets again, stopping when my lower legs are hanging over the edge. With a gentle nudge, he pushes them open.

For a split second, I worry that he's going to want to go down on me again. Give me an hour or two and, yeah, I'd let him. Now, though? I'm too tired and too sensitized from my orgasm.

Before I can tell him so—or he can sense it through our new mate bond—he gets the most determined look on his face. It's one I'm used to, one he always pulled when I was a kid and my shadow man thought he knew best, but now he's wearing it as he…

As he…

"Nox? What are you—"

"Every drop," he rumbles, using one of his shadow claws to scoop up his come and push it back inside of me. "I'll make sure my mate takes every drop of her male."

Oh. Okay, then.

Know what? I'm going to have to get up sooner or later. I'm going to have to get a washcloth and clean up the both of us. But with Nox's load dripping out of me and my insistent mate watching my pussy with such a look of possessive pride, I decide it can wait a little longer.

Anything to make my new mate happy.

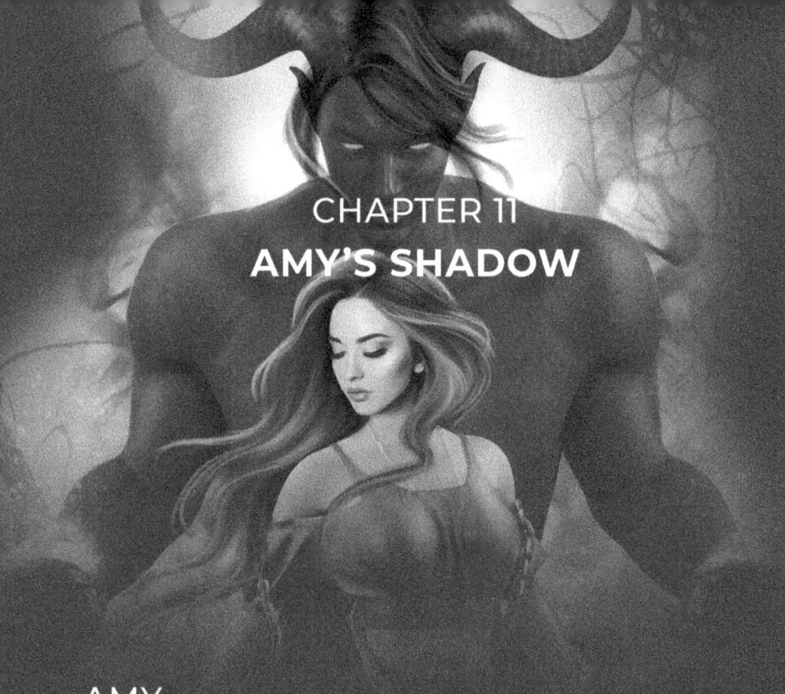

CHAPTER 11
AMY'S SHADOW

AMY

I missed my bed.

It's not even mine—not really, since it came with the apartment—but after spending one night outside, sleeping on top of a pile of garbage bags, I'm so glad to be sleeping on a real mattress.

Even better? Is having Nox right next to me, getting some rest of his own.

Turns out that Sombra demons don't need anywhere near as much sleep as humans do. I'm okay with six or seven hours. Nox, as a trained hunter, could get by with three or four hours every few days and not lose a step. I'm pretty sure he didn't get a wink the entire time we were hidden in his shadows. After everything we did yesterday and last night, I was happy to see that he knocked out shortly after I did.

I peeked. Half-dazed from pleasure—and, okay, twinging a little from the aftermath of our vigorous mating—I woke up after about an hour. I got up to pee and tidy myself, then I spent a good fifteen minutes just watching Nox.

My big shadow man snores. It was freaking adorable.

He also flexed his fingers, searching for me. His eyes were closed. During his sleep, he'd gone from a brawny, red-skinned demon with shadowy claws and a size-changing cock to completely inky black. He wasn't mist, so I could still feel his body against me, but that was the first time I've seen him with his eyes closed. Without the blazing red color, he was pure shadow.

He also looked strikingly gorgeous without the hint of danger that peeks out of his fiery gaze…

Nox reached for me, sighing softly when the tips of his blunted claws found my thigh. I'd risen up on my knees, sitting on my heels as I watched him sleep peacefully. He was my mate, and he already gave me his express permission to touch him whenever I wanted to.

So I did. I'd stroked his hard jaw, tucking his hair behind his slightly pointed ear. Still asleep, he leaned into my palm. A ghost of a smile whispered across his face as he sighed again.

And, I thought as I scooted down to cuddle next to him, if I hadn't been a hundred percent sure I made the right choice in tying myself to him for the rest of eternity, that would've done it for me then and there.

He's not sleeping now. As I stretch myself awake, I see that it's Nox's turn to watch me as I snore. He's still laying next to me, only he's moved so that he's on his side. His horn is digging into the wall between the rails of the headboard, leaving some sheetrock and paint chips on his pillow and in his messy hair. He doesn't seem to mind. All of his attention is on me.

Do I blush? After last night, it seems kinda ridiculous. I mean, a mate is like a wife. The mate's promise is an unbreakable vow that basically means we're married in the demon way. Shit. My pussy was all over his face, and his cock… it was inside of me. His come, too. I won't have to worry about a pregnancy scare or anything like that—a Sombra demon's seed is only fertile during the gold moon in his realm so we're in the clear there—but after how close we got last night, I shouldn't be so embarrassed by the way he's watching me with such an expression.

He's not blinking. His glowing red eyes don't shutter at all, almost as if he doesn't want to miss a glimpse of me. His lush lips are curved around his fangs, a look of pure male pride mingled with something… something soft.

Adoration. My big shadow demon, with shoulders twice as wide as mine, claws that could eviscerate any threat, biceps bigger than my head, and a cock that couldn't quite fit until we figured that out... he's looking at me as if I took the moon from the sky and gave it to him.

Better yet, I gave him my essence. My virginity and my heart, too. In my vow, I gave him *everything*, and he's watching me as if he can't believe his luck.

I can't believe mine, either. Maybe a normal human chick would see a towering demon with horns, fangs, claws, and—depending on his shape—red skin or wavering shadows and freak out. I could see them racing for the nearest church, looking for some holy water to try to send him back to his realm... not me.

I'm the girl who didn't even pour the salt circle like my aunt's handwritten notes told me to. It seemed silly to nine-year-old Amy, to spill salt like that, especially when that was something that seemed to upset my mom. As a kid, I thought it was because she had to clean it up. Only now do I see those idiot cop's claims that she might've been part of a cult or taken by Satanists with a new eye.

She had to have cast the spell. True love, right? What are the odds that Aunt Su was also the fated mate to a Sombra demon? That thought's one I've had a couple of times since Nox appeared so suddenly into my life two nights ago. While he still refused to let me out of his shadows, I asked him about other human-demon matches. As far as he knew we were the only ones.

As far as he knew...

On the plus side, now that we're mated, our lifespans are matched. After all, a Sombra demon only gets one true mate. It wouldn't be fair if they were fated to be with someone who had a fraction of their lifespan. That would be like sentencing Nox to an eternity of loneliness after I died. Now I won't.

We're mates. We have all the time in the world to discover everything that we didn't already learn from each other's essence.

That thought has me grinning up at him.

"Hey, baby."

Jeez, my voice is throaty. Kinda raw, too. Oh, boy. Just how loud did I get last night?

I didn't want to flush. I didn't want to be embarrassed about anything I did with this magnificent male. But… yeah. My cheeks are on fire.

He grins. "Good morning, my mate."

Hang on—

I blink. "Did you… did you just speak in English?"

A wicked grin splits his lips. "I have your essence now. I know everything about you, including your human language."

I squeal in delight, throwing my arms around whatever part of my mate I can reach. From my position curled into him, that's about half of his wide chest. It's enough for me to give him a tight squeeze.

It worked. The essence exchange, the sex… we did it. We forged a mate bond that'll never be broken.

He's mine now, and I don't have to worry about those other demons taking him away from me again.

Yes!

Sidling close to me, my demon wraps me up in his arms. I melt against him, just wanting to hold him close. We're going to have to talk about what happens next. The future as I see it, and what he expects from me now that we're mates—

Wait a second.

I just realized something. Nox is wrapping me up in his arms. And his chains? They're gone.

When I fell asleep, curled up next to Nox, he'd had them looped around me. He let me use his bicep as a pillow, too, so the hard metal of each link didn't cut into my skin, but they were definitely there during our mating.

They're not anymore. Come to think of it, I'm pretty sure they were missing when I got up to pee. I don't remember seeing them when I snuggled up against him, though I was too distracted by sneakily ogling my gorgeous demon mate. I was staring at his face, not his hands.

One of his hands is so big compared to mine that I need two of mine to grab his. I tug him, absolutely sure that the only reason that I'm able to pull him toward me is because he allows me to.

Don't care. I need to see this.

His arm is red. His hand is red. His fingers are red. His claws are black, though they're not shadows at the moment; when they touch the back of my hand, I feel their point. His wrist, though? The black marks I noticed the other night have returned. Three inches all the way around, it looks like it's the exact spot where the heavy manacles of his chains sat.

They're gone, but the mark is still there. Now that I'm looking at it closer, I see it's not black like ink. Nope. It's… it's his shadows. He's not doing that on purpose, either, not like how he can change the shape of his cock or blunt his claws.

"What happened?" I ask.

Nox flexes his fingers. He doesn't take his hand back. I get the feeling he wants to, but he doesn't. "When I broke the chains in the duke's dungeon, the manacles burned me all the way down to my shadows. It's the only part of me I haven't been able to heal."

"So… what? Is it always going to be like this?"

"Yes." It's a short answer. His jaw goes tight. "Does that bother you?"

Why would it? "No." I pause for a moment, then ask, "Does this have something to do with what happened with the car last night?"

"You mean how my shadows failed me and I was pulled under the vehicle?"

"Exactly."

"I believe so. Can't know for sure unless I talk to one of the duke's mages, but I had to feed a lot of my essence into the chains. I don't think I'll ever be the demon I used to be because of it."

Because of the chains—and because of me. How can he ask if it'll bother me? I'm not the one who was *burned.* Connor scared the shit out of me by showing up so unexpected. That's the most that happened to me. But Nox… he sensed my terror and put himself through life-changing agony to get to me.

What else is there to say except for… "I'm so sorry, Nox."

"Don't be. If anything, I should be the sorry one. You deserve a better male than the one the gods gave you."

That's bullshit. I rub my thumb over the mark. "I deserve the male I got. Besides, it's not like we can do anything about that now. We're stuck together, you and me. That's how the bond works, right?"

"Together," murmurs Nox. His breathing picks up, eyes gone heavy-lidded at my snapped words and my soft caress.

I don't know how he does it. A second ago, I was annoyed that he thought he wasn't good enough for me. Now? My body begins to respond to his. He's getting turned on and, well, so am I.

Huh. I guess mating my demon has made it so that wanton Amy gets to stick around for a bit. Because I'm about two seconds away from shoving Nox to his back and finding out what it's like to impale myself on his cock.

Nox almost chokes on his next breath.

"You okay, baby?"

He gives his head a jerky nod. "I am, but if you keep thinking about climbing on top of me, I'm not so sure how much longer I will be."

I blink. "Why… why would you say that?"

"Because I can scent your cunt getting ready for your male. And I *know* you, my Amy. I know your thoughts. Your essence is teaching me more and more about you, just like it's meant to. You want to mount me. I'm more than willing. I told you. I'm yours."

I don't know what to say to that one. Mainly because he's right, and because the primal way he grunts out 'cunt' like that has me squeezing my naked thighs together.

It would be so easy to take him up on his invitation. To straddle him and do all the things I'd fantasized about before I even knew it was my shadow man I was thinking of.

We have forever, I remind myself. Eternity.

And I still need a shower desperately. Breakfast, too, but shower first.

Giving him a quick peck at the corner of his mouth, I scoot away before he can lash his hand around me, dragging me back to bed.

Nox groans.

I giggle.

I freaking *giggle*.

"Mating later," I promise. "I washed up last night, but I need a good scrub. You're probably hungry, too." He refused the candy I offered him, and unless he went back for the rat, I don't think he's eaten since he's been in the human world. Big guy like him, he's probably starving. "I'm going to take a shower, then start some food for us. You can shower then, okay?"

In Sombra, most demons bathe. They have running water—and I don't even want to try to figure out how… more magic, I guess—and prefer oversized tubs; or, in Nox's case, dips in the hot springs of their heated realm when he was on an extended hunt. My apartment doesn't have a tub, just a shower stall, but Nox is intuitive. He'll figure it out.

I might have to show him how to handle the knob with his claws, though. My nails are basically nubs and it took me longer than I want to admit to figure out how to get it going after I moved in.

Once I'm off the bed, Nox's growl follows me into the bathroom. Wanton Amy gives her ass a little wiggle before I turn the light on and step into the room. His growl only deepens while I giggle again.

Pulling open the glass door, I turn on the shower, waiting for it to warm up. Once it does, I step inside —and discover that it wasn't only his growl that followed me.

Nox joins me in the shower.

I step back to give him room before tapping him on the belly. "Wow. You really are a shadow, aren't you?"

Laying his hands on my waist, he lifts me easily so that I'm on my tippy toes, perfectly positioned for him to bend his head and kiss me. He does, and then he takes one hand back. He's still strong enough to keep me right where he wants me as he hooks his claw around the edge of the glass shower door. He closes it behind him, leaving the two of us to stand under the shadow spray together.

It's a tight fit, but like last night, we manage.

Once the door is shut, he uses his claw to tilt my chin back. Water streams off of his horns, flattening his hair around his face. His eyes gleam as his lips curve.

"Where you go, my reason, I'll be there. You have yourself a Sombra male. I will always be *your* shadow."

Is it the rumble? The heated look? The earnestness in his tone, or the heat pouring off of him as he reaches for me again? Honestly, it's probably all of that—but, most of all, it's Nox.

When Connor chased me, I felt trapped. Stalked. Hunted.

But when my mate promises he'll always be there? I think of the years we lost while he was in the dungeon and I was all alone… and I want to hold him to it—almost as I want to just hold him.

BREAKFAST IS A HIT.

I fry up two packs of bacon, plus a dozen eggs.

That normally would've been enough to last me a couple of weeks. For a Sombra demon, it's one meal.

He refuses to eat first. As his mate, he insists that I do. Only when I tell him that I can't have another bite does he finish off the spread. Ten eggs and a pack-and-a-half of bacon… now that he's going to be staying with me for a while, I'm going to have to start budgeting for his appetite.

That's one of the things we discuss over breakfast and after, when I lead him into the living room instead of back to bed. Nox seems more than keen to give mating another try, but now that the cloud of lust has faded some, we need to think about what's going to happen next.

I kinda figured he'd suggest going back to Sombra. It's his home world. It's what he knows, and what he's used to. What does surprise me? Is how readily he agrees when I counter with the two of us sticking around the human world a little longer.

I must be a better lay than I thought.

Of course, then my noble demon has to go and ruin my puffed-up pride by reminding me that he already told me that he'll follow me wherever I go. So long as we're together, he doesn't care where we are.

It's not a lie. Whether he can't lie to me or he just won't, I know he's not lying to me. He honestly means that. Still, his endgame is keeping me in his home in Sombra, with a spawn or two as we grow our family.

We talk about that, too. For me, the decision to

mate Nox was a no-brainer. It was inevitable. *We* were inevitable. But kids… I'm only twenty-six. He's freaking twelve hundred. We're only just starting our life together. I like the idea of it just being the two of us by ourselves for a while.

When Nox agrees to that, I'm not surprised. Not this time. My shadow man spent fourteen years hoping for his lost mate, sure that we'd never be together. Now that we are, he gets growly when I leave his sight. I think he's more than content with some alone time.

I'm sure his possessiveness and overprotective nature will fade in time. It'll have to. Now that I know what happened with the car—when Nox lost control and shifted forms where anyone could've seen him—wasn't a fluke, we can't risk that happening again. The only one who can see him is me, and we gotta keep it that way. That means there will be times when I have to leave him behind and he's going to have to deal.

Just like I'm going to have to accept that I chose to take him as my mate. He can't help it if he's hard-wired to keep me safe. It might be a little smothering, but that's something I'll have to deal with myself.

Good thing that I don't mind.

I get my first taste of it throughout the afternoon. I try to encourage Nox to look around the apartment, to get used to it. Nope. Every time I turn around, he's right there. His expression grows more heated as the day goes on. Lunch distracts him, but by the time it's closing in on four, I start to wonder if it's too early to turn in.

And that's when someone starts knocking at my door.

Nox wasn't expecting the sound. He jolts, going from his demon form to a mass of shadows in an instant. I hold up my hand, signaling for him to stay where he is, then walk over to the door.

A quick peek and, surprise, it's Francesca again. Only… she's not alone. She has—

She has Spider-Man standing next to her. Holding a bright orange Halloween pail in his hand, I realize she must be bringing her son around to start trick-or-treating.

Crap. How could I have forgotten?

Candy. Where's the candy?

Kitchen.

"One sec, Brendon. Cool Spider-Man costume, by the way," I shoot over my shoulder as I dash for the kitchen.

I'd moved the bags of half-eaten candy and chocolate bars into the kitchen this morning. Grabbing a big bowl, I dump both in there, then give it a quick shake. There's a Butterfinger on top. I grab it and, returning to the door, drop it into his Halloween pail.

"Thanks," he chirps.

Francesca looks me up and down as her little

hellion starts off for 6D. "You in costume, Amy?" she asks pleasantly. She is. She's wearing a puffy pink dress with silver stars on it. Her red hair has been curled, with a weird-looking crown on top of it. A wand is clasped in one hand, a cell phone in the other. Throws off her Glinda the Good Witch costume a bit, but I've been seeing more and more people clutching their phones lately instead of leaving them forgotten in their purses like I do.

Glancing down, I look at the sleep shorts and the old college hoodie I'm wearing. On the one hand, I could play it off like I was a sorority girl or something. On the other, Francesca seems like the kind of neighbor it's just easier to appease.

And her costume has given me an idea.

"I will be," I tell her. Then I smile. "And I've got a guy friend coming to help me pass candy out to the kids. His costume… trust me. It's awesome."

Mainly because it isn't a costume…

"I'll have to stop by after we hit a couple of more floors," she promises. "I can't wait to see it."

I can't wait to see her eyes bug out of her head when she gets a peek at Nox.

I know that, by mating Nox, I'm looking at a lifetime of secrets. I won't be able to introduce him to my mom. We won't be able to go out together, to the movies or on a dinner date. I could care less. I rarely did that stuff before, and only when my ex made me. It's not that big of a difference.

But if there's one night that anyone can see him and they won't know that he's a Sombra demon, it's Halloween.

As long as he agrees to go along with it, this is going to be one the neighborhood kids will never forget.

CHAPTER 12
SAMHAIN

NOX

It's Samhain. Not just the season. The night.

I knew it was approaching. Without the veil between worlds going thin during this season, I'm not sure I would've been able to answer my mate's instinctive cry out for me. That also means tonight is when the gold moon rises. I thank the gods that my Amy bonded me to her the night before. So consumed with keeping her away from any threats, I hadn't realized that the deadline to make her mine was far shorter than I would've thought.

Now there is no deadline. I'm free from my chains, and they can't take her away from me. Once the mate's promise and our essence are exchanged, and my mate opens her body up to receive my seed, our souls are intertwined. It's right there in the vow.

They might separate our bodies, but they can never tear our souls apart.

I just hope that the duke will show mercy on me again. By mating Amy, I did what I couldn't all those human years ago. So long as no other mortal learns about Sombra, maybe I won't have to return to the dungeons. I'll never cross planes with Amy if that's to be my fate, and though I agreed to stay with her in this world until she's ready to visit mine, if it means I never have to worry about losing her, I'll abandon my realm for her.

The human world isn't so bad, after all. It's a little… complicated. In Sombra, magic takes care of most of our needs. What we can't use magic for, we all have a specialized skill. I'm a hunter. We have clan builders, clan artists, clan cooks… everyone does their part.

I'd forgotten about how different the human world was. Most likely because, when I visited it previously, I never left Amy's quarters. Once we could communicate, everything I knew about this realm was either from legend or from the eyes of my future mate. I admit now that I basically know nothing.

That's already been changing.

I already know to stay away from the wheeled vehicles. The squeaking meat I hunted is something akin to the beady-eyed shadow vermin that lurk on the edge of Sombra. I've eaten my fair share of ungez when bigger meat was harder to find, but Amy admitted that while she eats meat, she gets it from a… 'grossery' store, I believe. Rat—the fresh meat with the tail—is not something humans eat.

Having Amy's essence makes it easier to understand our differences. I try not to rely on tapping into her memories because I'd prefer to learn of my mate on my own, but I can't help it. As my mate, I know all of my Amy.

She dreamed of me. Whatever Sammael did to her after I was chained, he did as he said. I was nothing but a dream, though as she matured, her dreams became… naughty. Convinced as she was that I was a fond memory—no, something from her imagination—she fantasized about mating me.

My chest puffs out when I think of last night. I satisfied her better than the shadows of me that lingered in her mind. And I know it's ridiculous to be jealous of oneself. I don't care. I want our mating night to be the one she remembers the fondest.

I also know what that human male did to scare her so. Taking what she didn't want to give, stalking her like prey when she told him that she wasn't his mate… forcing her to believe that she'd never be safe, all while I suffered in silence in the duke's dungeons?

He deserves a fate worse than mine. He deserves to know what it's like to be hunted.

Only… she doesn't want me to hunt him. I gave my word that I wouldn't before I knew the truth of how he terrorized my mate. I'll stand by it because I love my Amy, and I trust her. Hurting her would cause me indescribable pain. While I would take it gladly, I will never, ever hurt her.

Even if I don't understand the tricky way that her mind works, I do as she requests. A devoted male does, and though we've only been reunited for such a short amount of time, I scoff when I think of the male I was mere days ago.

As if I could use my might and strength to convince her of anything. My Amy might be a wee creature, but she's more powerful than I am. Soft yet brave, kind yet unwavering. Her ex-mate is a threat to her; still, she spares him and shows him the mercy the human didn't grant her. Quiet and thoughtful at times, she knows what she wants and she goes for it.

I love it. Despite the hardships she's had in her life —the ones I see, and the ones I can only guess are hidden deep within her essence—I still see sparks of the child who amused me as I told her what it was like to be a Sombra demon.

She's mature now. No doubt in my mind about that. I may have seen many more years than my mate, but we are both frozen at our peak. She is my bonded mate as of last night—and, yet, she retains a childlike wonder that only makes me feel more protective of her and her innocence.

Samhain is an example of that.

In the human world, it's called Halloween. A spiritual season where neighboring planes bump up against each other, the humans have turned it into a celebration so different than anything we host in Sombra. Demonkind share feasts and stories of their ancestors, those who tired of an eternal life and either begged for execution or moved on to another clan or to another plane to start their life over.

Then there are the lost souls of Sombra. Those who were too cowardly to face the duke and ask for his mercy and his aid to end their lives. A demon could walk into the shadows that lurk on the furthest recesses of our realm and face the true monsters there. Feral beasts and carnivores who feed off of the same game I hunt, they'll also devour any living creature that goes too deep into their domain. It's a terrible death, since there are cruel beings that will use a demon's regeneration to feed on him for centuries, but those who enter the beasts' shadows are usually closer to becoming the monster in the dark themselves than staying an honorable Sombra demon.

There are elements of the human celebration that are the same. Amy showed me after the red-haired human female walked away. Here, she has a lantern made of an orange fruit. She used a knife to cut a face into it, then dropped a candle inside. In Sombra, we use the ancient horned skulls scattered near the shadow's edge to frighten the spirits away; we, too, put fire inside of the skulls if only to make their missing eyes glow. We had our own feast. She served me a bread and cheese delicacy from her world while we waited for the children's arrival. Pizza. No meat, and the stringy cheese clung to my fangs, but Amy licked them clean for me so I was pleased with the meal.

Then the spawn do arrive, and I see just how different Halloween is from Samhain.

With their parents standing nearby, the tiny humans knock on the door to my Amy's home. She opens it, cooing over their coverings. Instead of dressed in usual human tops and bottoms, they're decorated. Amy says they're wearing costumes and that, if anyone marvels over my appearance, I should tell them the same.

It's not a lie, she insists. They won't ask if I'm a demon from another plane, and I shouldn't offer. But if they compliment my demon form, it's only because they think I'm dressed up like they are. They can see me, but they won't know that this is how I appear when I'm not in my shadows. If they think I'm human like them, I'm not technically breaking the duke's first laws.

Ah. It seems as if my smart mate also knows a loophole when she sees one.

Amy traded her clothes for a black covering similar to my shadows. It falls to her knees, leaving much of her leg on display; I try not to stare and fail, especially since her feet coverings have her growing right before me. Her dark eyes are outlined in kohl, her hair spilling down her back. She says she's a witch if anyone asks after her costume, though most are just interested in the bowl of candies she's holding when she answers the door.

It's some kind of exchange. The spawn mumble the magic words and my mate rewards them with a treat. To seal the contract, the spawn thank her, then scamper off to another door to perform the same trick.

When I was in my shadows, I watched from a few steps away from the doorway. However, as soon as my powers fail and I'm solid again, Amy drags me by the arm to stand with her.

Before long, she hands me the bucket. She gets delight when the knock sounds, I open the door, and the children see me standing there.

I don't quite understand it, but if it makes her happy, I will follow her traditions.

Though I thought she had plenty of candies, the bowl empties quickly. I point out it's because the same children keep returning. Amy smiles and tells me they are, but it's because they want to visit me again.

I don't understand that, either.

She loots through the kitchen, bringing everything with her that she thinks the spawn will accept as part of their contract. One of the bright red bags catches my attention—Doritos, it reads, and it's my mate's favorite—and I pluck it from the bowl.

"They can have everything but this," I tell her solemnly. "This is for you, my Amy. Your preferred snack."

"I can get more," she says, a touch of humor to her voice. "There's always the store."

There is. And though I won't be able to accompany her once the magic of Halloween is done, I have to accept that, by joining my life to my mate's, there are things about living in the human world that I'll get used to. Shopping instead of hunting is one. Leaving her to watch herself when I can't is another.

However, I will never stand by and watch my mate hunger. What if she gives away all her food before she can find this 'grossery' store? No. I am her male. I shall provide for her, even if it's stealing a bag of Doritos from her nearby clan's spawn.

"I must," I rumble, moving the bag over to the furniture. "For you."

Amy rolls her eyes, though she does rise up on the tips of her toes, offering her mouth for me to kiss. I do so gladly, only snarling a little when there comes another knock at the door.

She pats me on my chest. "Go on, baby. It's your turn."

I nod, then reach into the bowl for my next treat. "Of course."

"The spawn act like they're frightened," I muse later as Amy closes the door once more, "but they don't have the fear scent attached to them."

The decorated human children smell like a variety of items, I noticed. Some are sweet, like my Amy—though none as sweet as my mate—while others have a spicier scent. Some are muddy, as though they've gone too long without bathing, and the smaller spawn are nervous until I use one of my claws to drop candies and other treats into the buckets and their bags.

"That's because it's Halloween. Being scared… or pretending to be… that's part of the fun, baby."

My cock twitches. All night, whenever I glimpsed my Amy's behind through her tight coverings, it was all I could do not to tear it off so that I could get back inside of her cunt. Only knowing that she was enjoying the Halloween festivities as much as the spawn kept me on my best behavior.

When the last knock came, she mentioned it was getting late. To me, that seemed like mate talk. Like she was preparing for us to return to her bedding. It could be, though I understand that Amy was referring to the hour. The Halloween contract only lasts for a few hours, she explained. The spawn should be returning to their own dens by now, gobbling their candies and removing their costumes.

I want nothing more than to do the same for my mate...

Her eyes light up. Courtesy of our mate bond, she knows exactly when I'm full of need for her. Now that

Halloween is coming to a close, I also sense that she's achy for her male.

There's barely anything left in her treat bowl. With a heated look that has Amy's scent perfuming with that delicious lust of hers, I drop the bowl on her furniture, then snag the Doritos. I plan on keeping my mate beneath me for as long as I can, pleasuring her until all she does is mewl my name. She might need sustenance after I make her squeal, and I shall provide it.

"Come, my reason," I begin, already crooking my finger to her. "Let us—"

The room darkens. The bright lights in Amy's home are still on. It's the sudden shadows that dim the space.

Only… they're not my shadows.

I'm thrown back into the past so quickly, I only have one reaction. Like she's a child again and I sense a portal ripping through the space in front of us, I bark at my mate to hide.

When Amy was twelve, she did. Tonight? She moves into me, laying her hand on my arm. "No."

I throw back my head and roar.

"Cute," she says, "but the answer's still no. We're in this together baby. Whatever's coming, I'm right here with you."

There's not enough time to cover her in shadows. Even if I had full control of my abilities, Samhain makes it so the portal opens much faster than it normally would. Before I can do anything, there's a black hole near Amy's door.

And stepping out of it? Is a demon I hoped never to see again.

"Glaine," I growl.

"*Glaine.*"

Next to me, Amy's dark eyes seem to flash as she repeats the soldier's name. They don't glow like those of a demoness, but the fire in her expression has me torn between wanting to toss her behind me so that she can't challenge Glaine—or hefting her over my shoulder so I can bring her to our bed.

No, Nox. Not now.

First, I must face Glaine. There's no Sammael with him—probably because Duke Haures knows the cursed chains can no longer hold me—but Apollyon, my old clan leader, is hovering behind the duke's head soldier. Apologetic as ever, I know that this isn't a friendly visit.

This time I do snag Amy by her arm, pushing her behind me. Then, rising up to my full height, showing Glaine that I'm the bigger male, I bare my fangs at him.

"You will not have her."

CHAPTER 13
AUNT SU

AMY

Glaine is a jerk.

And maybe I'm not being fair. All I know about the shadow with the curved horns and glowing green eyes is that he works as the duke of Sombra's head soldier. Since Duke Haures has to stay in his demon realm, whenever there's trouble off-plane, he sends Glaine. That's why he was in my bedroom all those years ago, telling Nox he was bringing him back to Sombra. He's a really high-ranking errand boy for the duke.

Nox doesn't like him for the same reason. I can tell. He respects the soldier's abilities, and thinks they're wasted serving the duke. Plus, he's still harboring a grudge over Glaine giving the order to have him put in chains and dragged to the duke's dungeon. It doesn't matter that he was only doing what he was told. Glaine is the male he associates with his imprisonment.

Me, too. And when his feelings mix with mine, I want him out of my apartment.

Before I can attempt to kick him out, my protective mate eases me behind him, putting his bulk between me and the inky black shadowy figure that is Glaine. The other demon has golden rune-like characters traveling down a pair of thick arms. Travel magic. Someone opened a portal for him to hop over to the human world, the evidence hovering over the edge of his dark form.

I can make out some details; not as easily as I can Nox when he's in this shape, but some. His hair is longer, his horns thicker at the base with a narrowed point that makes them shorter than Nox's. He has a pointed chin and a long nose, and those eyes… if Nox's remind me of 'stop' on a traffic light, Glaine's mean 'go'.

They flash, going impossibly brighter as Nox's voice drops to a menacing snarl. "You will not have her."

Glaine scoffs, though he doesn't make a move forward. He's a big demon, just not as big as Nox, and he doesn't have someone to protect like my mate does. I can feel him on the other side of our newly cemented bond. Nox will turn his claws and fangs on his fellow demon if he has to, if that's what it takes to keep me safe.

I can't let him. It does something to me to know that I have him in my corner no matter what. Not denying that. Still, Nox already spent fourteen years in the dungeon for me. What will the duke do to him if he decides to challenge and fight his soldier?

I don't know, but it doesn't matter. It's not going to happen.

"What do you want?" I demand from around Nox's big body. I lay my hand on his arm again, a silent signal to my mate that I got this. "What are you doing here?"

Glaine's haughty expression gentles a little when he looks past Nox, gaze settling on me. "I have my orders, female. The duke knows that Nox broke free of his chains and escaped from his cell. He wants him brought back to Sombra to explain himself."

"What about that guy?" There's a second demon. His name pops into my head. Apollyon. That's all I got right now. "Why is he here?"

He starts, almost as if he hadn't expected me to call him out. I don't know how. A little stockier than both Glaine and Nox, he's still a head-and-a-half bigger than me. The edge of his shadows might blend with the soldiers. He's still obviously there.

"I am Apollyon," he says, introducing himself. Yeah. I know that part. "I am the clan leader for the demons of Nuit. I'm here to stand for my clansmen."

Oh. Kinda like an advocate, I guess.

Fair enough. "Me, too. I don't know what your duke wants with my mate, but we're bonded. If he goes, I'm going with him."

Nox's head jerks over his shoulder. "Amy, no—"

Glaine clears his throat. "The summons calls for your human mate to come, too. Duke Haures insists. You will both accompany me back to Marvo."

Well, that makes this whole thing a lot easier. I thought I would have to argue and push and plead to keep the demons from separating me from Nox. I don't have the book with the spell that summoned him in the first place. It disappeared a couple of years after she did. Since I wasn't supposed to have stolen it from my aunt's house in the first place, I never asked my mom if she knew what happened to it. Without it, though, I couldn't try to bring Nox back—and I have no idea how to open a portal on my own.

If he disappears into Sombra without me, I'll never be able to follow him. And as absolutely positive as I am that Nox would stop at nothing to get back to me, how long would it take? He's only been in my life for two full days and already I'm addicted to him.

I can't go back to life as lonely Amy. Looking over her shoulder for an ex I never wanted, working from home, only talking to my mom once a day or, when I got really desperate, calling Laura just to hear someone else's voice. Now that I know what it's like to love, to *feel*… I can't go back.

And I refuse to lose Nox again. He might've been my imaginary friend once upon a time. Not anymore. He's my lover. My mate.

Mine.

He exhales roughly. I'm still holding onto his right arm. Nox lifts his hand, rubbing his naked chest with the heel of it. A pulse of pure need and affection hits me, burrowing deep into my chest. He felt my claim to him, and he's returning it.

That makes me bolder than I've ever been. Tilting my head back, jutting out my chin, I glare daringly at the other two demons.

"Well? What are we waiting for?"

I'VE NEVER BEEN IN A PORTAL. WHEN I WAS A GIRL and Nox visited me every few weeks, he also arrived in a swirling vortex of black shadows. If I was paying attention to the corner of my room where he usually appeared, I could catch a glimpse of Sombra before he came stalking through, but I never got the chance to see how one worked for myself.

Not surprisingly given that it's a shadow realm, it's dark. There are two moons in the sky: a black one, and a golden one. The dirt is dusty and red. Skulls litter the landscape, fire pits lending most of the light to break up the gloom. It's hot. Dry. If I got too close to the portal, the heat slammed me in the face. It seemed like the kind of place that's been in a drought for millennia, and when we could finally communicate in Sombran and he told me tales of his home, I learned I was basically right.

At least, in the part of Sombra where he lived, it was like that.

Nox was living in Nuit when we met. He was born in Fonce, and stayed in that clan for the first five centuries of his life before moving on to Nuit to be their hunter. Nuit was on the edge of Sombra, where the shadows that sustained his race of demonkind turned dark and deadly, becoming a kind of trap. Monsters—real monsters—lurked there. So did plenty of creatures that the Sombrans considered delicacies. It was the perfect part of their realm for a hunter to prove himself, and Nox was the most revered—and feared—hunter in either of his clans.

I've never been afraid of him. Not even when he first prowled into my room, nostrils flaring as he sniffed me out. When the portal initially opened, I'd crawled under my bed because I had no idea what was happening—only that the gigantic shadow man definitely wasn't my Aunt Su. But once he found me, crooking his claw at me and cooing softly in Sombran, it didn't matter that I had no clue what he was saying. Something about him made me feel safe instantly in his presence. He never scared me then, and as we're hustled into the portal with Apollyon and Glaine flanking us, I'm not scared now.

I think they are. If not scared, then leery of Nox. It's like they expect him to attack—which, yeah, fair. I have his essence and my bond with him makes it so that I can sense his emotions. He's itching to lash out. To show his might. The only reason he isn't is because I'm here, and he absolutely refuses to jeopardize me.

The actual travel is pretty quick. I have my hand clutching onto Nox's bare side. Like the others, he's in his shadow shape, so I'm probably squeezing harder than I should so that I don't lose him. He doesn't complain. Instead, he drops his arm around my shoulder, huddling me close.

By the time we're moving through to the other side of the portal, he's holding my weight. The four of us step out of the portal. I'm hovering a couple of inches off of the ground, thanks to Nox. Only once he's sure that we're clear of the portal does he set me down on my heels.

I don't know what I expected. I knew we were coming to see Duke Haures, but I had a long-held idea of what Sombra looks like. Every bit of it is from glimpses through the portal, Nox's stories, and now his memories. He'd never been to the duke's palace before when I knew him last, and most of his time in the dungeon he keeps blocked from me. I walked into this situation completely unprepared.

First of all, we're in some kind of elaborate room. The tile beneath my feet is slick and surprisingly cool. Sconces are lined up on the dark walls. No electricity here, so there are no lightbulbs. The duke doesn't need them. Each sconce has a ball of blue light spinning over the gilded decoration.

When I think of Sombra, I think of red. I've seen the red dust through the portal. Nox's eyes are red. His skin in his demon form is red. It's hot like hell, and that's red to me, too.

This space is blue. The strange light gives everything a slight blue cast. The golden decorations twinkle with it. The crystalline tile under my shoes is dark blue. The high ceiling is a paler shade, broken up by strategically placed circular holes cut into the space. Gold light filters down from the moon I can just kinda make out from my spot below it.

Finally, I turn to look at the massive gilded throne I consciously avoided as I swiveled my head, taking the room in—the throne, and the demon sitting on the seat. He's not alone. Next to the throne, there's another demon in his shadow form. This one has purple eyes, and I know immediately that he's the third demon who came for Nox all those years ago.

Sammael. The duke's mage.

The male sitting on the throne is the only one in his demon form. As if that didn't make him stand out enough, his appearance does.

In the light, I can't tell if his skin is white or a very, very soft blue; one thing for sure, it's not red like Nox's. He has pale hair the same color that he wears long. It falls down his back, past his broad shoulders. His eyes are a glowing blue, his fangs curving up from the bottom instead of overhanging his lower lip. He has a small crown tucked between his impressive horns. The rest of him is huge, too. Built like a linebacker on steroids, he's even bigger than my mate. Maybe it's his size, maybe it's his aura, but he seems far more of a demon than any others I've met so far.

No wonder he's the one in charge. Even if I didn't have Nox's essence to tell me who he is, it's obvious.

Duke Haures.

As soon as he sees that he has all of our attention, he rises up from his seat. With a grand wave of his hand, more royal than his monstrous appearance would suggest, he gestures to the demon standing to the left of me.

"You're released from your duties, Apollyon."

Apollyon bows his head deeply. "Yes, my lord," he says, then immediately dissolves into a mist.

I'm wondering why for a moment before I see it for myself; at the same time, Nox's memories make me understand what exactly I'm seeing. The mist that used to be Apollyon contracts, forming a tube, then blasts off like a rocket. He aims for one of the holes in the ceiling, disappearing from sight in seconds.

Whoa.

No wonder they don't have any kind of cars or vehicles in Sombra. Why, when they can travel so much faster in their faintest shadow form?

Once Apollyon has left us, the duke turns to Glaine. "Go and retrieve Dagon."

Glaine nods. He leaves, though he takes a side exit to do so. A door is built into the wall behind us, so seamlessly I didn't notice it. Shifting to his demon form—Glaine, I notice, is red-skinned like Nox—he stalks away, disappearing just as quickly as Apollyon.

That leaves me, Nox, the duke, and his mage all watching each other closely.

For now.

I don't know who Dagon is except his name sounds way too close to 'dragon' for me to feel comfortable. Neither does Nox. Between the blank in my thoughts when I see if his essence recognizes the name, and the way he hunches next to me as if anticipating a threat, I'm not so sure I want to meet this other demon.

Or maybe that's because he's growling under his breath as he stares over at the duke.

The duke doesn't seem so concerned. Makes sense. When he can sentence Nox to the dungeon on a whim—or worse—he has nothing to be worried over.

Me? I'm terrified. Because I know that there's no hiding that from Nox, I try desperately to control myself. It's tough. I'm not so sure I manage.

Luckily, the duke takes pity on me. "Be at ease," he says to Nox. "I have no intention of sending you back to the dungeon. Now that you've bonded to your mate, it would be cruel to do so."

"Then why are we here? Why did you send Glaine to retrieve me?"

"Is that what you think? I thought I made it clear. I summoned your female, knowing you would come along with her."

Nox glances at me, then looks over at the duke. "What do you want with my mate?"

"Me? Nothing. But my mate has been longing to meet her."

"Mate?" Nox sounds shocked. "Since when do you have a mate?"

Better question: why does his mate want to see *me*?

"Longer than you," is the duke's curt reply. "Of course, you'll understand that I refuse her nothing. But she had to wait until your bond with your human was final. I love my mate desperately, but I'm also responsible for all of Sombra. I couldn't invite a human into our world until I was sure she was one of us."

Huh. I guess I am part demon now. Not in any of the cool ways, of course. I can't fly like Apollyon just showed off, and while I can hide in Nox's shadows, I'm still completely human. I'm no longer a mortal, though. Nox's essence has changed me enough that I can visit Sombra and it won't get either of us in trouble.

You would think I would've figured out who

exactly Duke Haures's mate was. Later on, I'll admit it was super obvious. But just then, as the door opens and two demons escort her in, I never expected who the pretty brunette walking into the throne room would be.

There's Glaine. The other demon—with red eyes, just like Nox—must be Dagon.

And, cushioned between them, is… is…

"Aunt Su?"

Susanna Benoit, my mother's younger sister, was twenty-eight when she disappeared. Ten years younger than my mom, she was the cool aunt who doted on me my whole life; at least, until she was gone. A couple of years ago, the authorities declared her legally dead. Once they did, my mom took down any pictures of her that we had up around our house. It was as if it hurt too much for her to look at them, and I understood. I missed my aunt, too.

I remember what she looks like, though. I don't need a picture for that. Mainly because… well, she looks like me.

Her hair is longer than I remember. The same shade of brown as mine, it's just as wavy even as it reaches the small of her back. She's the same size, with a curvy build highlighted by the simple white gown she's wearing. She has a gold necklace hanging low, nestled between her boobs, and a hesitant yet friendly expression on her face.

She folds her hand in front of her belly. "I've been wanting to see you for a long time, Amelia."

"Amy," rumbles Nox.

I lay my hand on his arm. Like before, it instantly calms him. I appreciate the thought and I make sure to send that through our bond. I am Amy—but this is the aunt I haven't seen since I was eight.

And she looks as if she hasn't aged a day.

Duh. I mean, obviously, right? That's how bonding with a demon works. Whether you were immortal before or not, when a demon creates their unbreakable bond with their mate, their lifespans match. What did I expect? That I'd continue aging and, eventually, be a shriveled husk and still be alive because of my tie to Nox? Of course not. From the moment we bonded, I'll forever be the same.

Just like my Aunt Su is now.

"Is this… are you really…"

"Susanna?" she supplies. Her dark eyes glisten. There are tears there. "I am. I… you're all grown up. I can't believe this."

Neither can I.

I guessed. I mean, it was a pretty logical assumption. My aunt was gone, leaving her book behind, and then I read from it and met Nox… yeah. I thought she had some tie to Sombra. But the duke? Sombra's ruler who, from Nox's experiences, always seemed so anti-human?

That's a bit of a shocker, not gonna lie.

"I know. There's so much I want to tell you… so much I want to explain." Her eyes flicker to her mate. When he nods at her, she exhales softly. I'm shocked, but my aunt is nervous. Her mate's solemn nod seems to calm her enough for her to blurt out, "Would you like to come and talk to me in the garden? I understand if you don't, but…"

There is no 'but'. Do I want to find out what happened to Aunt Su all those years ago? And see what a garden looks like in Sombra?

"I'd love to."

Her pretty face breaks into a smile. "It's right this way."

"Dagon," calls out the duke. "Watch over my mate and her kin until I can relieve you myself."

The red-eyed demon nods. "Of course, my lord."

I start toward her. Behind me, Nox shadows my step. Of course he does. My mate won't let me out of his sight.

Until the duke stops him, that is.

CHAPTER 14
THE DUKE

NOX

"Don't."

Of all the beings in Sombra or on Earth, there is only one who can command me and I will instantly obey. That, of course, would be my mate. However, when Duke Haures snaps out the one word in the human language, it's enough to startle me into pausing.

It's a message for Amy and me, possibly his mate as well. No one else in his chambers would know English because they do not have a human mate. At least, not that I know of. The reveal that the ruler of Sombra has kept his human mate hidden in his castle for as long as I've known of my Amy is something so unexpected, I begin to wonder if there are hundreds of mortals spread out all over Sombra with their demons.

I don't think so. Nuit might be a poorer clan, far from Marvo, but if humans were no longer considered forbidden fruit, I would've known. When Glaine came for me the first time, he made mention of the fact that I was the first Sombra male in centuries who was fated to have a human mate.

Centuries, he said, but this female is Amy's kin. The reason why I met my mate in the first place. And that was about a decade-and-a-half ago…

There's a book. Amy showed it to me once, though it didn't really interest me. It might have once. The leather-bound spellbook—a magic grimoire from thousands of years ago—belonged explicitly to the Sombra mages during my lifetime. Only a select few demons had the magic to read the spells and work them. I wasn't one of them. I'm a hunter, not a spellcaster. It didn't matter that the spell for summoning a mate was in the book if I couldn't read it, and by the time she showed it to me and I could've bartered with a mage to cast it, I already had my mate.

Full of magic and life, my wee human had read the spell and summoned me to her side.

Humans are so very different from demonkind. Because their mortal life is so short, they have an entire existence crammed into less than a century. Their essence, I've discovered through Amy, is quite strong. Even as a child, she read the spell and because fate chose us for each other, she found me.

But I was not the soul she was searching for. The book, she eventually explained, belonged to her mother's sister. Her Aunt Su. She had carried the grimoire everywhere, constantly trying to translate Sombran into English. At some point, she must have figured out how because she was able to understand the *verus amor* spell.

She must have cast it, too. Cast it and found that she was the fated mate to the most powerful demon in all of Sombra…

She didn't disappear. She stayed with her male in Marvo.

Her true love.

That's what *verus amor* means in English. True love. Her aunt had marked up the summoning spell in pencil—only that one spell—and Amy thought that meant something. So she read it, hoping to see her aunt again, and she got me.

From that moment on, our fates were sealed. I may have had to wait longer than I hoped to—thanks to the duke—but I always knew she would be mine.

And nothing… *no one*… will take her away from me.

I take a step toward Duke Haures. Glaine moves to stand at his side. Behind him, Sammael raises his arms, already conjuring something between his palms.

Three against one. Four if you count the guard

standing with Amy and her kin. With Amy's essence flowing through me, and no chains to weaken me, I'm prepared to rip through all of them to make sure my mate is safe.

She knows, too. And, before I can take another step, she calls out to me.

"Nox, baby." Her sweet voice cools the fire raging inside of me. "It's okay. I'll be right back."

"My reason," I begin, turning toward her. Like a moth drawn to a flame, when she wants my attention, I'm helpless not to give it to her. Thankfully, the reassuring look on her pretty face extinguishes the last of the heat. "You'll return to me?"

"Of course." Her gaze flickers to her aunt, a touch of nerves—nerves and excitement—coloring her scent. She then glances past me, nose wrinkling as she looks at Duke Haures. "I promise. You're my mate now. We came here together. We're leaving here together."

The duke meets her stare. Instead of threatening her with the dungeon, he bows his head. "Your visit to our realm is a favor for my mate. I have no intention of keeping you in Sombra if you'd rather return to Earth."

"Hear that, baby? It's gonna be fine. I'll talk to my aunt. You talk to your duke. We'll be together before you know it."

I hope so.

With a flick of his claws, Duke Haures gestures to

both Glaine and Sammael. "Go with Dagon. Leave me with Nox."

I can tell that neither of his soldiers is happy with his order. They don't question it, though, and immediately join the human females and the other guard. At another signal, they leave, slamming the elaborate door to the throne room behind them.

Odds are one on one now, I can't help but notice. I don't charge, only because my mate wouldn't want me to, so I plant my bare feet against the chilled tile below them.

"I swear to the gods, I'll do anything for my mate. I proved that when I broke the chains you kept me bound in, and when I escaped from your dungeon." No point in not confessing to those crimes. I'm sure that duke already is aware. "I sacrificed everything to get to her, and that was only when a promise of a bond existed between us. She's accepted me as hers." She claimed me in front of the duke and his mate. "Nothing will keep me from her. Not even you."

Then, to cap off my words—all of it in Sombran because I don't care who might be listening and can hear—I tilt my chin, angling my horns so that the points are high and directed at the duke.

Should I have shown defiance to Duke Haures now that we're alone? No. I do so anyway. To another Sombra demon, it's a challenge.

He lifts his hand. "Lower your horns, Nox."

I refuse.

Duke Haures's pale blue eyes deepen until they're purple. With a sigh, he slams his hand in a downward motion.

My head jerks so quickly, my chin slams into my chest, my fangs biting deep into my flesh. Blood fills my mouth, the rusty tang catching my attention before the pain does.

I spit out a curse. The duke simply raises his eyebrows at me.

"Behave, Nox. I'm not your enemy. This eve, I'm not even your lord. Your duke. I am Haures. And I understand."

I swipe the back of my hand against my chin, wiping away the blood dripping down it. That's about all I can do with my head stuck like this.

He gestures. I can swivel my head on my neck again. Without showing off my horns or my fangs, I glance over at him a lot more warily than I have before. So Duke Haures also is a conjurer. Something else no one in Nuit knows.

"What do you mean, you understand?"

"Susanna is mine." His pale eyes—glowing blue again, no hint of purple at all—glance toward the empty doorway. "I guard her ruthlessly. I understand what a treasure it is to call a human your own."

I want to ask him why he threw me to the dungeons. I don't. I already know the answer. When Amy's kin disappeared into Sombra, she was mature. Amy wasn't. Simple as that.

"I know how it feels to be willing to tear the worlds apart for your mate. I made my laws long before I knew a human female would own my heart. She's here because we abide by them. Because she chose me. Because it isn't easy to have a mate who isn't a demoness. Who is other. Especially when you have an entire realm relying on you to protect them from the danger of mortals."

I can't even argue with him. I have Amy's essence. Most mortals…there's a reason why I'd rather her come live with me in Sombra. Connor still scares her, but he's not the only dangerous mortal she's known.

And let's not forget how an innocent male was dragged beneath one of their vehicles all because he traded shapes at the worst possible moment…

"She's safer with me. Susanna knows it. I *am* Sombra, so she stays here knowing she'll never be able to return to the human realm again. When you left the dungeon, it was clear you went for your mate. Forgive me, Nox, but that's exactly why we called you home. Susanna is mine, but she's no demoness. She trusts me. She loves me. Still… your mate is her kin. She had to be sure that your time apart didn't make you another danger to your Amelia."

"Amy," I correct. "She's my Amy."

Duke Haures bows his head again. "Yes. Amy. Susanna knows how far I will go protect her. She needs to hear from your mate that you're equally as devoted."

That's no problem. My mate knows she's the reason I breathe every day.

But the duke… "And how far will you go?" I wonder.

"Only those loyal to me know of my mate's existence. Any who threaten her… they don't earn the dungeon." His white face goes dark with barely caged fury. "They're left to the shadows."

It's the harshest punishment in our realm, and one I never expected the duke to confess to. *Guard her ruthlessly…* it seems that he does exactly that.

The edge of Sombra's shadows is littered with skulls. Nuit is one of the cities set far from the capital of Sombra, much closer to the end of our realm. I've spent the last six centuries among the skulls. For a world that has existed for thousands of years, with a people who are immortal, there weren't so many that it drew any attention. Like the dry earth and the beasts in the dark, they were just there.

But the pile grows. I assumed it was from those who searched out an end to their life. Now I know better. Duke Haures is responsible for a few.

I've never liked our ruler. As a hunter, I only begrudgingly respected those who provided for their clan like I did. Living in his castle, setting law and tenets from a gilded throne… I thought little of him. Less when he had me thrown in the dungeon.

Until I see him for what he is. A demon fate chose

to lead, and a male as obsessed with his human as I am.

Hands folded behind his back, Haures waits to see my reaction. I give him none.

Why? Because I'd do the same for my Amy and he knows it.

There's a solemn understanding between us. No more posturing. No threats. None are needed, and I know without a doubt that, once Amy is done talking to her kin, Duke Haures will give us free passage back to the human world. So long as I follow his lead—so long as I continue to abide by his rule and ensure that no other mortal discovers Sombra demons exist—then we no longer have to worry about dungeons or chains or shadows.

I feel a weight lifting off of my shoulders. One that's been there for so very long. Taking a deep breath, I shudder out the relief I feel.

The action catches the duke's attention. He nods again, then lifts his hand once more. Instead of controlling me, though, he uses the claw on his pointer finger to gesture to his chest.

Specifically, he points to the silver runes that spell out Susanna's name.

"One thing more, Nox, before I leave you to wait for your Amy." He taps his chest. "You're mated now. Prove it."

CHAPTER 15

GRIMOIRE DU SOMBRA

AMY

"Wow." I spin around, taking in the garden. "This is amazing."

The door led us right outside. The ground is big slabs of stone, with a small pond on one side, and a giant circle full of hundreds of different types of plants of flowers. It smells like I've walked into Yankee Candle, the scents are so different yet so strong. The golden moon leaves a shine over everything, especially the water rippling on the pond.

It's cooler than I expected, too. If I didn't know we were still in Nox's hellish world, I'd think I'd just gone through another portal.

"Marvo is an oasis," explains my aunt. "It's the capital of Sombra where Haures has his palace. The rest of the world is more like a desert, but not here."

She walks over to the flowers spilling out of the center. Plucking one with a pale blue petal, she brings it to me. "This is the only spot in Sombra where you can see this color."

"The duke seems pretty fond of blue."

"Haures… he's always appreciated the rarity in life. When you live as long as he has, you have to find something to keep things new."

I don't think I'll ever get a better opening than this one. "Like a human woman as a mate."

She nods. "That's right."

As easy as my aunt is to agree, that's all I get out of her for the moment. Instead, tucking the flower behind her ear, she moves back to the slight stone wall containing a majority of the flowers. She sits down gingerly, folding the skirt of her white dress beneath her, then taps the spot by her side.

Thanks to my form-fitting dress, it's a little more awkward for me to join her, but I do my best.

At her curious look, I feel the need to explain. Or maybe it's just that, after seeing my aunt after so long, the quiet is just as awkward and I have to fill it.

"Tonight was Halloween," I tell her. "I needed a last-minute costume." I gesture at my over-the-top make-up, the black dress I bought for those fancy date nights with Connor I couldn't avoid, and my three-inch heels. "I went witch."

"Fitting," she says, smiling. "You cast the *verus amor* spell."

"I did, yeah. Back when I was a kid."

Her smile wavers. "I know."

I figured.

But then she blurts out, "It's my fault. I've waited all these years to tell you… I'm so sorry, Amy."

What? "Why? Because you disappeared?"

My aunt nods. "That, but also because, if it wasn't for me, you never would've been able to cast the spell. Not that I'm saying you shouldn't have. I love my mate. I'm sure you love yours—"

"I do." I have to make that clear. "I love Nox."

"Exactly. But not when you were a little girl. When I first heard from my mate that another of his subjects was summoned by the spell, I'd hoped… I'd hoped the book was found by anyone else. Obviously not Mindy"—Mom—"because of Dan"—Dad—"but… I didn't want it to be Amelia. You were so little when I left."

True. "I grew up," I tell her. She might look the same, but I don't. "Mom, too. After you disappeared, she spent so long looking for you, hoping you'd come back, Dad left." Honestly, it's a shame she didn't summon a Sombra demon of her own. He would've treated her better than my deadbeat father did toward the end of their marriage. "I'm glad I had Nox for company, even back then. Other than Mom, he's all I had."

"Dan… left? He left Mindy?"

You know something? Living in Sombra, I

honestly think that Mom's sister thought the world would go on without her.

Hardly.

"They were divorced by the time I was nine. We moved to Madison to be close to your house… that's how I got the book."

That's how I got Nox.

"I didn't…" She exhales softly. "I'm sorry for that, too."

"Don't be. Dad's a dick."

Aunt Su chokes out a laugh. Her eyes go wide. "You really did grow up, didn't you?"

"Yeah. I did. It wasn't easy." Especially since I spent fourteen years believing Nox wasn't real. "But I did. And I mean it. You don't have anything to be sorry for."

"You're wrong about that. Dagon?"

"Yes, mistress?"

I raise an eyebrow at that, but Aunt Su continues as if that's not weird at all.

"Can you get my book for me?"

"Of course."

He waves his hand. A patch of shadow appears in front of him. He thrusts his hand into it. When Dagon pulls it out again, he's clutching something between his claws.

When he begins to to hand it to my aunt, she shakes her head. "Not me. Give it to my niece, if you would."

My mouth falls open as I accept the book from him. Up close, I can see that my initial suspicion was right. It's my aunt's old book.

"I thought I lost that!"

Aunt Su's expression turns sheepish. "You didn't. I asked Haures to have one of his soldiers slip into the human realm and take it back for me."

"You didn't have to do that. If Nox asked for it, I would've sent it with him. I didn't even need to know you wanted it." Like Dagon, I try to hand it to her. She draws away from it. "It's a Sombra book. It should stay here."

Tucking her hair behind her ears, she shakes her head slowly. "I thought so, too. But I was wrong, Amy. It needs to be in the mortal realm. It needs to find a human who's fated to be with their demon."

"Like me now."

"Yes. Like you."

If that's so… "Then why did you take it?"

"Because you were a kid," she says, tossing my own words back at me. "I know what it's like to be a demon's mate. I wouldn't change a thing about my life… but I wanted to save you from yours. Taking the book wasn't enough. It just told me I was right when I thought you were the mortal being shadowed by one of Haures's demons. So when he touched you… I convinced my mate to put him in the dungeons."

I… wow. That was the last thing I expected her to say to me. "You did?"

"I had to. Sometimes one touch is all it takes. If you gave him the mate's promise—"

"I didn't. Not until last night."

"I know that now. But I was worried. My little niece… even in Sombra, I wanted to help keep you safe."

That's the funny thing. "Nox makes me safe. He always has."

"I don't regret what I did. Fourteen years sounds like a lot to a human, but I thought he could wait for you to grow up. You have, Amy. He can keep you safe now. I won't interfere again."

Good. I'm glad we got that settled.

I lay the book in my lap. "Okay. In that case, I'll hold onto the book, but only if you answer my question first."

"Of course. Ask away."

I've got hundreds more questions to ask of Aunt Su, but this one has bothered me for longer than I want to admit. "You have got to tell me why the cops found chalk and salt on the floor when you disappeared…"

We talk for hours more.

I'm not even exaggerating. Dagon leaves us for a little bit, bringing back a tray full of demon wine and some kind of meat that—remembering the rat—I pass on. When I wonder why, Aunt Su explains that we've missed dinner and the duke refuses to let her go hungry.

I already satisfied my curiosity about the scene Aunt Su left behind, then had to admit that I didn't bother with the protective circle when I accidentally manifested Nox. I confessed I'd hoped it would be her coming through the portal—making her smile waver —since I never, ever thought I'd conjure a shadow monster.

She does laugh when I tell her that the first thing I remember asking Nox is, "Are you the bogeyman?"

But when she mentions her mate… the smile returns. Every single time.

So, though I already know the answer, I have to ask her. I have to hear it for myself.

"Are you happy here?"

"More than I can put into words," is her quick answer. "Haures might be the duke of Sombra, but he treats me like his queen. I might also regret how I got here, and how I could never explain where I went, but this was my fate." She reaches out, patting my thigh. "I'm just so glad you found your own fate."

Me, too. "So… you can never go back home?"

"This is my home now. It has been since I followed my mate into this amazing world. Haures… he belongs in Sombra. I belong with him. I can't go back. That life… it's not mine anymore."

I figured. She's been here for almost twenty

human years. That's almost as long as I've been alive. And, shoot. She has a powerful duke for a mate, a palace for a home, and a devoted guard who shadows her when Haures can't.

I asked her about Dagon the second he slipped out to get food for us. My aunt got a faraway look in her eye before shaking her head and telling me that he believes she saved his life. He vowed to serve her until he draws his last breath, or until he finds his mate. As loyal as he is, mates come first, and she whispers that she's hoping that he finds his female in a Soleil demoness during his upcoming trip off-plane.

I totally understand. It's one thing to have a shadow monster up your butt every second of the day because he loves you and wants to keep you close. To have one pledging to be your servant? Poor Aunt Su. She probably never gets alone time.

Dagon gives us our privacy; or, at least, some semblance of it. Knowing how strong a Sombra demon's senses are, he probably hears every word. That makes me careful in choosing how to answer some of my aunt's questions. Between her and her demon guard, whatever I say is getting back to Duke Haures. I have no doubt in my mind about that.

I still can't help but gush about Nox. After her confession, I want her to understand that I'm happy. Deliriously happy. And, sure, this might be the honeymoon stage following our mating, but my aunt tells me that it's common for mates to move quickly once they recognize each other. Demonesses and demons usually mate the same night, and even humans feel the pull of their bond.

And if they don't? Turns out mate sickness is real. I'm just super glad I never had to experience *that.*

The spellbook isn't the only thing that my aunt gives me. When I admit that I plan on sticking around the human world for a bit—which should be fine, she assures me, as long as no other mortal finds out about Nox—she asks about her house. She's not surprised to hear that my mom locked it up, leaving it for her even after Aunt Su was declared "dead". Just like she's sure that her older sister will never feel comfortable about staying in it instead of our old apartment in Madison.

She's not wrong. Mom offered it to me when I came back from college, but I didn't feel right moving in, either. We both kinda considered it my aunt's still —until Aunt Su tells me that she'd love it if I moved in with Nox.

What she doesn't say is that it'll be hard to keep Nox hidden in a Jersey City apartment. I only have one bedroom there, and very little space. My aunt's house is a ranch, but it's much, much bigger. For as long as we're still in the human world, it would be better for him—and without any pesky apartment neighbors nearby.

I give her a hug to thank her. I'll never be able to explain to Mom why I suddenly feel okay with the idea, but if I do move back to Madison, she probably wouldn't care. Aunt Su's house is a five-minute drive away. That's way better than three hours. So, yeah. She'll probably love the idea.

As I'm pulling back from her hug, she shifts in her seat. I follow the direction of her stare. Even before I see Duke Haures stalking into the garden, I know what I'm going to find.

The smile splitting her lips belongs to only one soul: her mate.

And, suddenly, I feel like I'm intruding.

The duke seems to think the same thing.

"Dagon, if you would bring Susanna's kin back to her male. He's waiting for his mate. And I… I miss mine."

"Haures." After patting my thigh again, she stands up, striding right toward him. As she meets him, he opens his arms up.

Aunt Su murmurs something to the duke as she steps into him. He folds her into his embrace, one arm around her back, the other cradling her head as if she's the most precious thing in the world to him.

She's his mate. She's gotta be.

I wonder… is that what I look like wrapped up in Nox's arms? Small and almost dwarfed by his bulk? Probably. I just hope I come across as happy to be there, too.

"If you would," murmurs Dagon. "This way."

I know a dismissal when I hear one. I get the vibe that this garden has special meaning to my aunt and her mate. They've already seemed to have forgotten all about me. It's like they're the only two in any realm who exist right now.

Yeah… that's my cue to go. Besides, I have my mate waiting for me.

Literally.

Nox is standing in the exact spot where I left him. He has his legs spaced apart, shoulders hunched, fingers flexed to make his claws as sharp and dangerous as possible. He growls softly when Dagon shoves the door open, blocking me from him. Once I step back into the throne room, he straightens.

And, just like that, we're the only two who exist.

"Amy," rumbles Nox.

Nox.

I start to hurry toward him, only stopping when about ten feet separate us. It takes until I'm that close before I notice there's something different about him.

It's his chest.

When I left him in Duke Haures's throne room a couple of hours ago, he was in his solid, demonic form. From his essence, I know that most Sombra demons assume that shape in their realm when they're among those they trust. They only go shadow during travel, when they need to heal from an injury, or when they want to prevent one. Or, of course, when they cross into another plane and they're avoiding any danger—or anyone seeing them that shouldn't.

Even though he shifted forms twice before I left

him to spend time with my aunt, he's solid again. There's no hiding the marks on his chest.

I'd noticed that Duke Haures had something similar. It was harder to see since his skin is so pale and the markings were a faded silver. Nox, on the other hand, is a deep-red color. The bright silver stands out.

Is that… is that a demon tattoo?

Welp, it's better than chains.

I want to ask him what happened while I was gone. I want to find out what his new tattoo means. Before I can try—or even tap into his thoughts and memories to figure it out for myself—he grabs my hand, tugging me into him. At that moment, I don't care how ridiculous we must look. He's a hulking demon. I'm a human woman. We fit perfectly, and that's all that matters.

I shudder out a breath.

He tightens his hold enough to comfort me. I don't know if he realizes what he's doing. Doesn't matter. This is right where I belong.

"I have you, my mate," Nox murmurs in my ear.

Yeah. He does, doesn't he?

CHAPTER 16
AMELIA

AMY

He holds me tight until we've passed through the portal again, bringing us back to my apartment. Even then, once I have carpet beneath my heels instead of tile or stone, I cling to Nox.

I don't regret getting to see my aunt. Now that me and Nox are bonded mates, I can return to Sombra with him whenever I want. I can see her again. Have a relationship. Learn more about what it's like to be mated to a demon from a human's perspective. As much as she obviously loves her duke, she seems as lonely as I used to be. I'd love to spend more time with her.

I also don't blame her for what happened. It's clear she thinks she's to blame for Nox's stay in the dungeon, and me not seeing him again until now. If I was in her situation, I would've done the same exact thing. A twelve-hundred-year-old demon believing my nine-year-old niece was the one true mate he'd waited his whole life for? I would've nipped that in the bud after one meeting. It took her three years because Nox was smart—and respectful. The duke knew he was seeing his human mate, but we had no real bond. He didn't touch me or give me any of his essence. I kept him a secret like he asked me to, and while he taught me about Sombra, nothing happened between us for the duke to interfere in one of his subject's mating.

Until Nox touched me. Until I pestered him enough to see what his shadows felt like, and he marked me. Duke Haures had proof he broke the first law then. Either Nox had to mate me or he had to be punished. I was only twelve. Of course he chose the chains.

The duke was looking for an excuse to split us up because my Aunt Su wanted him to. I get that. She took the spellbook back so that I didn't accidentally read the second half of the summoning spell that I initially neglected. Because: *surprise*. While the first part—the one I read that she had written "manifest" next to in her pretty script—was the spell that called Nox to me, the second half was actually the mate's promise.

If I had read it to Nox—even if I had no clue that's what I was doing—our bond would've been triggered when I was a little kid. I'm absolutely sure Nox never would've done anything, but what kind of life would I have had as a Sombra demon's mate that young?

I would've had to leave my mom. I never would've gone to college or figured out what I wanted to do with my life. Sure, Connor wouldn't have been an issue, either, but I needed that time apart from Nox to grow into the Amy Benoit I am today.

And this Amy? She's ready to be Nox's forever mate. I proved that when I mated him, and when I claimed him in front of his ruler. I might have gone off to talk to my aunt, but I knew I was coming back for Nox.

Now he does, too.

With a gentle nudge, I push against my mate. He releases me without a moment's hesitation.

First thing I do is kick off my high heels. Then, I head to the couch. The candy bowl is still laying there from where I tossed it what seems like a lifetime ago. I drop the spellbook next to it.

I'll have to figure out what to do with that. My aunt made it a point to tell me that it belongs in our world. After I thought about it, I have to admit that she's right. There might be a bunch of Sombra males who missed out on their human mates because there was no way to get to them. In accordance with the duke's two-thousand-year-old law, the spell only works one way. A human has to read it to summon their demon into Earth. Sombra demons are only allowed to cross planes into the mortal world when they're summoned, but if there are no humans left who know *how* to summon them, how can those demons find their mates?

The answer is in the *Grimoire du Sombra*. Aunt Su already did the hard part. The *verus amor* spell is translated. She even added warnings that, hopefully, smarter humans than I am pay attention to, like the protective circle with salt and chalk to keep the demon contained until the human understands just what kind of true love they summoned, as well as the warning about saying the 'promise' only when both mates are ready.

After talking to her, it's obvious my aunt is convinced that the spellbook itself is charmed to fall into the hands of humans who are fated to be with a Sombra demon.

Like her.

Like me.

There's no reason for me to keep it. I'm not interested in any other spells in the book, and I already have my mate. Who knows? Maybe there's a woman out there right now who doesn't feel like she belongs, and the only thing she's waiting for is a male like Nox.

Strong. Protective. Gorgeous.

Devoted. Kind. Loyal.

And did I mention sexy as hell?

Another chick might look at him and scream. Not

me. Everything about him, from his towering build to his incredibly lickable horns and that wicked tongue of his… I look at him and I'm ready to *cream.*

He knows it, too.

His nostrils flare. A rumble builds low in his chest. "Delicious," he grunts. "My mate… your lust is delicious."

My cheeks go as hot as the rest of me. One day soon I'll remember that his senses are way keener than mine. That I know he's primed to mate because there's no missing his hard-on—even when he's wearing shadow coverings like he is now—but he knows because he can scent me growing wet.

I know what he's thinking, too. He'd spent the whole day waiting for me to give him some sign that I was ready to mate again. Earlier, we got distracted with the Halloween festivities, then there was our impromptu trip to Sombra. With the duke basically giving our mating his blessing, there's nothing stopping us now.

Except for my curiosity.

I step into Nox. Without my heels, I'm even smaller next to him than before. I got used to at least reaching his pecs, though now I'm staring at his abs.

His abs, and the new tattoo he has on his chest.

I only got a quick glimpse of it before. Now, I get the chance to pay closer attention—and he lets me. Thrumming in place, fingers flexing as if he's dying to touch me again, he braces his bare feet on my carpet and sticks out his chest so I can't miss what's there.

My eyes see six characters. The first and the last ones are the same, with the other four runes different. They remind me of the golden runes that appear on the demon's inky forms after they've traveled from Sombra to Earth. The big difference is that these marks are a gleaming silver, and it looks like they've been carved into his muscular chest.

In the spellbook, the words are written in Sombran, though the letters are the standard alphabet used in English. Long before my aunt tried to translate it *into* English, another determined human must've translated it from these runes. Because, though I've never seen them before, his essence makes it so that I see runes, but I *know* what it means.

A hint of a smirk curves my lips. "It says 'Amelia'."

He's been careful to use my chosen nickname since I first corrected him in the alleyway. I don't know whether to be bemused or a little annoyed that he branded my full name on his chest like that for any other demon to see.

Because I finally understand. When I thought it was a demon tattoo, I was kinda right. In Sombra, they don't have weddings or anything like us humans do. You mate, and you're together. There's no cheating. No divorce. No reason to make a big deal of it, either.

Unless you're a male.

To show their entire world who they belong to, they mark themselves with pure silver. It's the only injury their shadows can't heal. He might have claimed me as his mate when we had sex the first time, but this is his way of showing that I own him.

And Nox proves it when he tells me earnestly, "It's the name that's been etched on my heart since I recognized you as my mate. It's only fitting that I wear it on my skin."

"What about 'Amy'?" I tease.

"You're my Amy. My mate. My reason… but you're also my Amelia."

Fair enough. I lay my hand on him, then trail my fingers down his arm. "I just like being yours."

Nox closes his eyes, shuddering beneath my touch. "Always."

Forever.

Seeing my aunt was awesome. To hear that she's happy, that she adores her duke as much as I love my shadow man… I'm glad I got the chance. That doesn't change the fact that, when I first saw Glaine appear in my apartment, I was terrified. Only now that I'm home, now that we're both back in the human world together, can I admit the truth to myself.

I can't take Nox's hand in mine. It's too big. Settling for wrapping my fingers around his thumb, I tug until his eyes blink open. The red gleam is so comforting that I find it easy to make my confession.

"I thought they were going to take you from me."

"I will never allow that."

I know. That's the thing, though. Fear isn't always rational. It's consuming, just like other strong emotions. Panic. Grief.

Love.

Letting go of his finger, both of my hands go to his chest. He inhales roughly, but goes still otherwise. He's proving again that I have complete control. That I can touch him where I want, when I want.

First, I want to explore his new markings. Fresh as they are, they rise up off of his skin like a welt. Folding my right hand into a fist, jutting out my pointer finger, I begin to trace the farthest "A" character.

We both know how this is going to end. As I move my finger along the silver, he begins to subtly rock his hips. He stops when I lift my finger from his heated skin, starting up again as I trace the "M".

My curiosity continues.

As much as his fully demonic form gets me going, when I think of Nox, I imagine him with his inky shape. He hasn't switched back yet, but that doesn't stop me from wondering…

"Can I ask you something?"

"Anything."

God, I love it when he grunts like that.

"Before… you said one of the demon mages in Sombra might be able to help you with your… switching issue." I trace the "E" with my fingernail. That added scrape has him going perfectly still again… or maybe it was what I said. Even so, that doesn't stop me from adding, "Did you get to ask one?"

He shakes his head, hair swaying with the motion before hitting his sharp jaw. "It's what I thought. Breaking the chains left me this way. In centuries, I might be able to stop my forms from changing on their own. Not now."

"What about if I… you know. Asked you to change forms for me. Is that still possible?"

I'm on the "L" now. It's a jagged rune, and he sucks in another breath as I quicken the pace of my stroke.

It takes him a moment to realize what I asked. I'm tracing the "I" as he leans into me, his voice gone throaty. "You mean like stealing you back into my shadows?" At my nod, he says, "Such as this?"

I shudder against him. I'm growing more sensitive to him. Before, I saw the shadows as a haze surrounding us. That's how I knew that he took me inside of him. Now that we're mates, I *feel* him. Is it his essence? Or what makes Nox *Nox*? I don't know. It doesn't matter. Being wrapped up in his shadows doesn't just make me feel comforted and safe.

I feel loved—and, okay, *super* horny.

After discussing it with my aunt—and wasn't that a bit awkward—I'd decided that it wasn't the mate sickness that had me coming onto Nox that night in the alley. Instead, it was a mate bond that had lain dormant for a good couple of years while I was a grown woman dreaming of my fated mate, and he was stuck in his charmed chains. Once we found each other again, the lust… the need… was undeniable.

Just like now.

"That's nice," I purr. "Not what I meant, though."

"Tell me, my mate. What did you mean?"

I reach the last letter in my name. This whole seduction thing would've been a whole lot quicker if he'd gone with 'Amy', but you know what? I'm not complaining.

Neither is Nox.

He's bowed over me, angling his hips back as if trying to hide how desperately he wants to bury himself inside of me. Since that's exactly what I want, I move until there's nothing separating us except for my slinky dress and his drifting shadows.

"Come here, baby."

He immediately drops his head down to mine.

Perfect.

Leaning in, my lips against his earlobe, I whisper, "I have a secret."

"Tell me," he grates out again.

"I always wondered what your shadows felt like."

"I know. That's what got us in trouble in the first

place, my mate. You were always asking me if you could touch them and find out if they were soft."

I tuck my face against his thick throat, grinning into his skin. "You remember."

"I remember everything about those nights we shared."

"Because I'm your reason."

"Because you're my *everything*."

Good answer.

"When I was a kid, I was more amazed by the way the shadows moved," I admit. "You're there, you're real, but the edges of you… I thought it was so cool."

"Ah, but I am a male from Sombra. I'm shadow and flame. I am not cool."

Could I love this guy any more? "You always have been to me. Hot and cool at the same time."

He ghosts his big hand over the back of my shoulders. "Just like you."

Just like us.

Now that we're mates, our essence entwined, his touch isn't as hot as it was. I'm not as icy to him anymore, either. We're perfect for each other.

"Yes, but you're still a shadow demon," I point out. Darting out my tongue, I swipe it along the side of his neck. "And now I'm wondering what it would be like to mate you when you're more shadow than demon."

For a heartbeat, I wonder if I inadvertently

mentioned some kind of shadow monster taboo. I thought that Nox would jump at the chance to mate again… but he doesn't. Actually, he doesn't do anything.

Oops. I messed up, didn't I?

You know, there's only so much help having Nox's essence can give me. This mating is so new, and unless I know the right kind of question to ask to pull up the answer inside of me, I'm bound to screw this up.

On the plus side, he mated me already. It's not like he can walk away because I didn't know demons only fucked when they were fully formed. Right? And, honestly, I should be forgiven for bringing it up. When he mated before, he turned his dick to shadows so that I could take him easier. Same thing with his claws. He blunted them so I didn't get scratched, so it's not like he was wholly demonic the last time.

It's not my fault—*whoa.*

Nox is strong. I've always known that. Fast, too. Still, when he hefts me up, tossing me over his shoulder while also ensuring that he's hoisted me high enough that it doesn't dig into my gut, you can definitely say I wasn't expecting that.

Or the way that he marches me into our bedroom.

As he lays me out on the bed, I can't help but grin in anticipation.

Maybe I didn't mess up, after all.

CHAPTER 17
SECRETS

NOX

Once I've laid her out on her bedding—*our* bedding—I rise up again so that I'm standing over her.

Her hair is spread out beneath her. I ache to run my claws through her tresses. It's so soft, and it smells so sweet, but that would be tending to my own pleasure first.

And my Amy has confessed that wants to know what it's like to mate with my shadows.

I'd never even hoped that she would offer. In Sombra, if a male found his mate in a shadow demoness, it was expected. Soleil demonesses, however, only have one form. A demonic appearance with golden skin, orange hair, deep brown horns, and a deep well of magic, they refuse to accept their mate's shadows.

There isn't much demonkind knows about the mortals. Duke Haures was able to take a human female as his mate and still there's so much legend surrounding the fabled creatures.

Amy opened herself up to me when she gave me her essence. I knew from that moment on that she was proud to have me as her male, and that she went into our mating sure that a future with me was what she wanted. What the gods and fate provided for us both.

But she's human. Like the females from Soleil, she has only one form. Solid yet irresistibly soft, I assumed she would only ever want to mate while I wore my skin. I don't look human at all, but this form was closer to what she'd known with her ex-mate.

Connor. His face flashes before my eyes and I have to work hard to stifle my growl. He has no horns. In a challenge, I could ram him without any fear of breaking one of mine. No claws, either, for the human male. I could skin him like I do meat, and he would never hurt my mate again.

Only… she doesn't want me to. So I'll respect her wishes, and I'll replace fantasies of what I would do to the human with what had me stroking myself during the time I was trapped in the duke's dungeon.

Mating *my* human while wearing only my shadows.

I crook my claw at her. As I don't trust my body to

not switch shapes so soon, I will myself to stay in my demon form for as long as I can. Until we're ready to mate, I don't want to fade to my shadows in case I change back while I'm inside of her.

She doesn't seem to care that I'm still standing there, big and red and waiting. Letting out a soft keening sound that goes straight to my cock, she pushes herself up to her elbows. Another crook and she's sitting on the edge of the bedding.

Perfect.

I hook my hands under her arms. She shivers at my bold touch. I grin.

Lifting her easily, I set her on her bare feet. Then, caressing her back, her waist, her hips, my hands travel past the curve of her ass until I've gathered as much material of her silky coverings as I can in my hands.

I don't want to tear her covering with my claws. When we were sitting on her furniture this morning, I left gouges and slashes in the material when I lost control of my claws. Gritting my fangs, I'm as careful as I can be as I start to wind the material upward, dragging it over her delectable little body.

Once she realizes what I'm doing, she helps. She lifts her arms over her head so that I can pull it off before dropping it to the floor.

She has the coverings on her breasts. Remembering what happened the last time I was faced with the delicate material, Amy reaches behind her, undoing them for me.

I cup her breasts in my hands, shuddering at how perfect they feel in my grasp.

"Nox…"

I squeeze gently, giving her a smile full of hunger and need. "Can I tell you a secret now, my reason?"

Breathless, she nods.

"My body responds to your touch differently, whether I'm in my skin or my shadows. The pleasure you give me like this is more than I'd ever hoped for. But when I shift forms"—as I do now—"the sensation is indescribable."

I'm only touching her breasts, but I feel the echo of Amy—of her essence—through every inch of my shadowy form. Like this, because of how she can skim through my shadows before reaching the denser parts, it's as though she's inside of *me*.

Just the idea of having my mate inside of me while I'm inside of her has me about ready to explode.

I won't be able to hold this shape long. I'd hoped I would, but already my sac is tightening. When she licks her lips, her dark, dim gaze going heavy-lidded with lust, I start thrusting against her belly. It would be a waste of seed since my Amy deserves every last drop I have, but I… I can't stop myself.

Until she drops her hands between our bodies and takes a firm grasp of my cock.

During our earlier mating, I guided her to grab onto my horns. It gave her leverage and kept her from sliding too far from me as I thrust into her. To my surprise—to my delight—Amy uses my cock to steer me back toward the bed.

And, gods, I let her.

She climbs up first, still gripping as much of my cock as she can. I only just resist the urge to buck into her fist. Through the edge of my shadows, the sensation of five, wee, claw-free fingertips has me groaning softly.

This is like pleasure I've never known before. I'm sure I'll think that every time I'm with my Amy, but this is different. This is new.

This is what I've waited twelve centuries for.

She knows it, too. With a smirk that I try desperately to kiss off of her face, she strokes my cock, sending even more pleasure to the base of my spine. My whole body jerks, but I guard my fangs as I take her mouth. It's harder when she exchanges her stroke for an insistent tug.

I rip my mouth from hers in time for her to lay on her back again, her naked body scooting toward me. Her legs are spread wide, her cunt perfuming the air around me. I lick my lips, savoring the taste of my mate's mouth, ready to feast on her cunt again.

"Uh-uh," she says, a tease in her tone and need in her eyes. "I still got this."

She squeezes my cock. Her fingers dig even deeper past my shadows.

A guttural sound escapes me. It might be her name. It might be a treaty to the gods. All I know is that I'm about to release all over her.

Ah. My tricky little mate has other ideas for me. As if she can tell—and, through our bond, she must—she angles her hips up, positioning me right at the source of her heat.

Mating is instinctive. The act, of course. Learning my mate and preparing for our future together is more difficult, but the pleasure of working my cock into her cunt… now that I know how pleasurably I can make the act for her and me both, I start to push.

She squeals.

I pause, halfway in. It's not the frustrated sound she let out when she was afraid we wouldn't fit, but I have to see that she's in no pain.

"How do you feel, my mate?"

"Amazing," she breathes out. "It tickles and it's making me super sensitive at the same time. And I'm pretty sure I can sense how good this is for you through our bond, too, so it's like double the pleasure, double the fun."

My mate often says the oddest things. But she says 'amazing', and I agree. "Take more, then."

"Oh, baby. I'll take it all."

That's all I need to hear. All I've ever wanted to…

"It's always been yours, my reason."

And it forever will be.

AMY

Two weeks into our mating, my biggest regret is that I can't tell Mom anything about Sombra.

Aunt Su made that clear. Duke Haures's laws apply to everyone, including his mate. It's not only his law, either. When he became ruler of his demon plane two thousand years ago, he created an alliance with the other realms. Soleil's one. So is a place called Brille Rouge. They all agreed to keep demonkind separate from the mortal realm.

I don't blame them. Humans… we kinda suck. I could just see it now. If we as a people discovered that there was another world we haven't colonized yet, we'd try. We'd take their resources and try to figure out how their magic worked compared to the technology we rely on.

Demons are immortal. How much do you want to bet some enterprising human would want to figure out a way to change that? Not because they were mass murderers, either, but because it would be a challenge some too-smart scientist would want to beat.

Oh, and we've got a bunch of murderers, too. Government-sanctioned ones, even. If the whole human world found out about demons, I'd give it days before somebody waged war on them.

So, yeah. I get it. I really do.

Does that mean it gets any easier to lie to her during our daily call? Not even a little.

When I hang up, my demon is always there to remind me why I've made the choices I have. A lot of the time he does that with his body—and when he can control his shape long enough to have sex in his shadows, it's even better—but that's not all. In the time since he's been back in my life, I remember exactly why I used to think of him as my imaginary friend.

Because that's what he is. Not imaginary anymore, of course, but a friend. My best friend.

Like those years when I was a kid, Nox loves to listen to me talk and tell stories. I was always the motormouth; I considered it a bit of a victory whenever I got him to do more than grunt at me. Of course, that was when we had no real way of communicating except for a really terrible game of charades. Determined to get to know my shadow man, I learned Sombran long before his essence would download the language into my brain. He talked a lot more then, even if I was doing most of the chatting.

It's so easy to fall back into that relationship. And, yeah, it's different now. Nine-year-old Amy had no idea what sex was, while twenty-six-year-old Amy can't get enough of her mate. But that's only a small part of this new relationship.

He still likes to listen to me talk. Though he knows all about my life from my essence, he wants to hear it from me. We have an uneasy agreement that I don't talk about Connor because it makes me nervous and Nox murderous, but nothing else is off-limits.

In return, he tells me about Sombra. As part of the same agreement, he skirts around his time in the dungeon. Instead, I learn more about Nuit, Nox's clan, and my aunt's mate. He makes living there sound so tempting, and though we still decided to stick around the human world for now, I don't think I'll mind visiting Sombra in the future.

Just gotta make sure he doesn't show me what his kills look like before he feeds me…

For now, while we're still in Jersey City, feeding us is my job. My kitchen isn't anything like what Nox was used to in Sombra, and I've been giving him lessons on how to use the oven and the stove, but I tell him it's my turn to provide for him.

And that includes going to the grocery store for plenty of food.

He hates that he can't come with me. He won't come out and say that, of course, but our mate bond makes it so that I know. Even if it didn't, I know Nox. He's not satisfied unless he's my shadow in truth. He wants to be able to follow me everywhere and gets frustrated when he can't.

If I was sure that he could control his shadows, I'd bring him with me every time I was forced to leave the apartment. In his faintest form, no one would be able to see him except for me, just like the duke's law insists. He can usually dissolve pretty easily, but as the accident with the car and the tire and the chains proved, he could also switch in the blink of an eye.

He points out that the chains are gone. And I get that. I'm glad they are. That doesn't change the fact that he could still appear in front of a bunch of humans. If that happens, it doesn't matter that we're bonded mates. Duke Haures will send his soldiers after Nox and then he'd have two new prisoners for his dungeon.

Because, no matter what, I'd go with him.

Nox understands that. He knows what's at stake. That's why, whenever I leave the apartment, he doesn't argue. He might pout a little—and it's adorable, the way my big, scowly demon pouts—but he always rumbles, "Come back to me, my reason."

And I always promise that I will.

The one downside to having a seven-and-a-half-foot tall mate—and, yes, I know he's that tall with horns because I freaking measured—is how much food he plows through. That first breakfast wasn't a fluke. He eats a *ton*. If I went to the same store every time I needed to do a grocery run, they'd think I'm feeding an army up in my apartment. That, or I'd clean them out of Nox's favorites.

I try to alternate between big grocery stores like ShopRite and the corner stores closer to my apartment. It's only been a couple of weeks so I haven't really drawn too much attention to myself… well, except for this little bodega a block from my apartment. I've gone from a casual nod when I walk in to an effusive, "Miss Amy," so… yeah. Might have to avoid that one for a while.

Not surprisingly, Nox is a huge fan of meat. If I cook a big roast with a bunch of sides, he's usually satisfied. I've had the hunk of meat for tonight's dinner in the oven for the last hour before I realized all we had were potatoes. I needed at least corn or green beans or something to go with it. Some bread. Then I thought about tomorrow's breakfast and added eggs to my list. Another roast, maybe even a practice turkey now that it's November.

Nox enjoyed Halloween. With his ravenous appetite, I think he'll get a kick out of Thanksgiving.

My local ShopRite isn't that far, but I always need my car for that trip. Between the distance and the amount of bags I'd have to carry back, it just makes sense. So I grab my keys, promise I'll be back as soon as possible, then dash out the door.

I shop as quickly as I can so that I can get back to Nox and, before I know it, I'm already back with a full trunk if a lighter wallet. My mind already up on the sixth floor of my apartment building, I pull into my parking spot in the underground garage. My building keeps a rack for moments like this. All I have to do is pop the trunk, unload my groceries onto the rack, and wheel it into the elevator. Within minutes, I'll be reunited with my shadow man.

And I think that all the way until a hard body pushes against my back, nearly toppling me into the open trunk I was leaning over. The rack beside me, I'd been reaching for one of the bags that had fallen toward the far side of it.

The edge of the trunk cuts into my belly as I gasp.

My first wild thought was that it was an accident. That someone swerved around the rack, bumped into me, and I stumbled forward. Praying it was an accident, I try to get up.

The weight of the other person keeps me down—and that's when I'm sure it's no accident.

I take a deep breath, prepared to scream.

Click.

Something cool. Something sharp.

Something *dangerous* is pressed to the side of my throat.

My scream dies before it can even begin, and a male chuckle takes its place.

"Ah, darling. I wouldn't do that if I were you."

CHAPTER 18
NOX THE HUNTER

AMY

Connor.

No.

I hadn't forgotten about him. As much as I tried to put him behind me so that I could focus on being with Nox, he always lurked in the back of my mind. I never stopped looking for him when I went out, and I've avoided the store where I bought the Halloween candy two weeks ago because I was terrified he might be waiting for me there.

But he wasn't. He's here.

How? I have no clue. The underground parking lot is for residents only. You need a passcode to get in. Unless he just walked in here, but if that's the case, what's his plan? Shove me in my trunk and drive off in my car?

If so, then what's pressed to my throat? Even worse, what is that bulge digging into the small of my back?

Holy shit.

No.

Oh, no, no, no.

This is it. My biggest fear come true. Connor found me, and four months after he tried to force me to sleep with him, he's back—and he already has an erection.

Because I'm bent over my trunk? Because my obvious terror is turning him on? Or because he gets off on holding something sharp to my throat, controlling me before I even have the chance to react?

He didn't whistle. I don't know why that strikes me as so ominous—as if this could be any worse—but it does.

He always whistles.

When I go impossibly still, he probably thinks it's because I'm being a good girl for him. I mean, that's obviously some kind of weapon. A knife? It's gotta be a knife. If I move… if I scream… I have no doubt that he'll use it, then convince himself that he had to. There was no choice. He gave me a warning, right?

He just wants…

"What?" I gasp out, trying to keep from losing it entirely. "What do you want, Connor?"

As much as I want to keep him from possibly slitting my throat open, it's more than that. My heart might have skipped a beat when I recognized Connor's voice, but it's fucking *pounding* now. If Nox felt my fear in another realm without us even being bonded yet, how quickly will he realize that's something is wrong when I'm only seven stories beneath him?

I can't let that happen. I just… I *can't.*

I think I surprised my ex. After what happened the last time we met, he probably expected me to piss my pants or something. I can't run like I did then, but I sound eerily calm for a woman at his mercy.

I have to remember that Connor thinks he's the victim here. Knowing him, he has probably convinced himself that this is something I pushed him to. If I'd just answered his calls and his texts, or I'd let my mom tell him where I'd gone, he wouldn't have had to resort to attacking me like this. Not once during our relationship did he think he'd ever done anything wrong. Why would he start now?

He's the victim. I'm the woman he controlled for too long. He doesn't realize how much I've changed since I left him—or how much he *hasn't*—which is probably why he figures it's a good idea to back off and give me some room to maneuver.

I take it.

Shoving off of the car, I nearly trip over my sneakers as I hurry to put a good six or seven feet between us. Only then do I dare look over at him.

First thing I notice is that he has an unfolded

switchblade in his hand. He might have backed off. He didn't conceal his weapon.

Still a threat, Amy. Remember that.

As I stare over at him, my hand flies to the side of my neck to check to see if he's already used it on me. Relief rushes through me when I pull it back and see that there's no blood. No nick or cut. Phew.

The dimple in his left cheek pops as he smiles at me. Cute. He thinks popping out of the shadows and threatening me with a blade is funny.

I'm not laughing.

"Come on, Amy. You didn't think I'd actually hurt you, did you?"

Of course I did. "How did you even find me?" I know my mom wouldn't have told him. "This is private property."

"That's right. But Jimmy is an old buddy of mine. When you sublet his place, he told me where you were staying. Made me promise not to confront you where his neighbors might see, but… look, darling. It's just you and me down here."

Right. As if I needed the reminder that we're completely alone. And Jimmy… fucking Jimmy. If I get out of this in one piece, I'm going to give Laura's friend a piece of my mind. She knew I was hiding out from Connor—so Jimmy probably did, too—and that jerk *sicced* my ex on me.

But, first, I have to get away from him…

"You don't have to do this, Connor."

"Do what? I was just trying to get your attention. Four months I've been missing you, darling. Two weeks since you slipped through my fingers… I had to do something."

"Why?" I probably should take the chance to scream. Only knowing that it would be a huge mistake to involve anyone else in my problems keeps me faking my calm. "What's so important that you won't just leave me alone?"

"What's so important?" he echoes. "How about the fact that I love you."

I want to hurl. "Connor—"

"You love me, too," he insists.

I never did. I can admit that. Deep down, I'm sure he knows, too. That's probably what made him such an obsessive stalker in the first place. I've told him 'no' since the beginning, but he wouldn't stop. I didn't want to date him. I didn't want him to spend nights in my room. I didn't want him to put my hand on his cock, or to push it between my lips.

I didn't want to sleep with him.

Every single damn thing I didn't want to do, he got his way if he pushed me hard enough—until that last one. That was the one that broke me, that had me fleeing Madison for Jersey City. The one that had me tossing my cell phone and looking over my shoulder way more than was healthy.

I don't love him. How can I?

Even before Nox, I knew I didn't. Now that I've seen how a man—a male—treats the female he adores, it's obvious that Connor never loved me, either.

He wanted me. I'll give him that.

Well, guess what? You can't always get what you want.

"You should just go," I tell him. My fear has turned to anger. Anger at Connor for even trying this. Anger at myself for letting him control me for far too long. I try to keep it back, but it's there as I say, "We can forget this happened. You can leave and forget all about me."

And finally… *finally*… I can do the same for him.

His jaw clenches. "I'm not going anywhere until you let me explain. Come on, Amy. Talk to me."

Talk?

Talk?

A hollow laugh escapes me. Talk, huh? Okay. Let's talk.

"The last time we talked, you had your hand around my throat and my pants around my ankles," I spit out at him. "You might have forgotten, but I haven't."

Connor frowns. Asshole has a knife in his hand, and the nerve to look like I hurt him with my accusation.

"You got it wrong, darling—"

"Don't call me that!"

Connor takes a step toward me.

Nope. I let him get too close to me too many times before. If he regrets letting me up, that was his mistake. He'll have to use that knife on me before I willingly let him touch me again.

His face darkens. His dimple's gone.

He rotates the switchblade in his hand. "Amy. Get the fuck over here. Now."

You know what? He said the same thing that night when he chased me into the alley…

Is that what does it? Or was it the sudden jolt of fear at the memory of that fateful night mingling with my emotions right now that calls my mate to me? I don't know, but Nox rises up from the shadows of the far reaches of the parking garage as though he'd been there the whole time.

He wasn't. I know that for sure. My fear summoned him and, damn it, that's the last thing I wanted to happen!

He might've been shadows. He's not now. Stalking forward in his fully demonic form, onyx horns angled toward Connor, eyes flashing furiously… there's no denying that he's a living, breathing shadow demon—and Connor is a mortal who was never supposed to set eyes on him.

I thought he hadn't before. When he chased me into the alley… I hoped the red eyes spooked him and he ran without putting two and two together that I was rescued by my shadow man.

But then Connor points at him with a shaky finger and cries out, "You… you're not supposed to be real," and I know otherwise. He saw him, only he convinced himself that Nox didn't really exist.

Welcome to the club, asshole. I didn't think Nox was real, either, but I'm glad he is.

I just… I wish he hadn't shown himself to Connor.

There's a law, and Nox just broke it. Would it matter if he came to save me in his shadow form? I think so. The duke didn't punish Nox for showing himself off to Connor when he lurked in the shadows.

Only now… Nox isn't lurking anywhere. He's striding through the lot, moving his big body so that he's positioned perfectly between me and Connor.

"You frighten my mate, human." His English is stilted, but I know he's using my tongue because he wants to make sure that Connor understands him. "I'll warn you once for her sake. Leave her be and never return and I shall spare you. That is the only warning you shall have. I suggest you heed it."

"Mate." Connor's handsome face twists into a look of disgust. Any fear of Nox he had—and should still have—evaporates as he realizes exactly what 'mate' means when Nox refers to me as his. He turns to me. "You?" he snarls. "And *that*? You wouldn't fuck me, but you let a… a monster stick his dick in you?"

To Connor, that had to be the last straw. Funny how he calls Nox a monster when he loses the last vestiges of his humanity as he raises his knife and charges at me.

Later, I'll wonder what he thought that would accomplish. Nox is stronger, faster, and more powerful than my ex; monster or not, he had to recognize that. My mate appeared from the freaking shadows to loom in front of him without any regard to the blade that was as big as one of Nox's fingers. He would have never let Connor get close enough to stab me. And if he managed to? I don't think all the 'please's in the world would keep Nox from gutting Connor in return.

He tries anyway.

He makes it two steps before Nox surges forward, clasping him by the back of the neck.

Connor is two feet off of the ground, legs still motoring before he notices that he's not going anywhere. Swiveling his head, his eyes nearly bug out of his head when he comes face to face with Nox.

"My mate doesn't want me to hunt you," he rumbles, turning to shadow. Connor lets out a yelp that Nox ignores. Golden runes pop up along his inky black arms as he uses his claw to slash a portal in the dark parking garage. "She didn't say anything about others doing so."

What? Oh. No. He wouldn't—

"Nox—"

—he would.

His red eyes flash. "Wait for me, my Amy."

I don't even get the chance to answer. Tightening his grip on Connor's neck, Nox lifts him easily, then disappears into the portal with my ex.

The echo of Connor's scream is all that's left behind after the portal winks out.

And I.. I burst into tears.

It just seems like the right thing to do. I'm crashing from the adrenaline spike that surged through me when Connor first grabbed me. The portal is closed, and even if I thought I could open it up by reading the summoning spell, I donated the spellbook to a library last week, hoping someone destined to find it did. I mean, Nox is mine. He never leaves my side. Why would I need the summoning spell?

Silly Amy. Maybe because there might have been a situation just like this…

The duke has to know. The way he's tapped into all of his subjects, I'm absolutely positive that he'll know that Connor saw him. Will that earn him another stay in the dungeon or, because it's his second offense, will he be executed?

Will I ever see him again?

Seconds pass, though it seems like an eternity. I stay standing in the middle of the parking lot, crying while my trunk is open and all my groceries are just waiting for me to do something. Oh, God. The meats… what will I do with the meats if Nox is gone forever?

My tears turn into full-blown sobs as I bury my face in my hands. That's what breaks me tonight. Thinking about the thirty pounds of meat I have in my trunk and no Sombra demon to eat it.

"Amy… don't cry. I am here."

Nox.

I choke on my next sob, head jerking up to see him hovering in front of me. He's fainter than normal, probably because of the power it took for him to create two portals, but he's there.

I throw myself at him.

Nox wraps me up in his arms. I can sense his puzzlement and despair that he returned to find me so distraught. I want to tell him that these are happy tears now, that I'd honestly believed for a few seconds that I would never see him again. I can't. I just blubber into his chest while he runs his shadowy claws through my hair.

It takes a few minutes for me to compose myself enough to face him.

"Nox… what?" My voice comes out raspy and thick. I swallow, then try again. "Where did you go?" And how was he able to come back?

"Don't cry, my mate," he says softly, using his claw to gently wipe away the tears from my eyes. "He might still survive the shadows."

I pound him in the chest. I don't know if it's out

of fear or relief or what, only that it feels right. "I don't care about him!"

I'm shouting. I probably shouldn't. Nox handled the Connor problem, but if one of my neighbors figures out I'm talking to someone and they notice Nox, we'll be in even more trouble.

Too bad I can't help it.

"You left me again. You said you'd never leave me. And for what? Wait..." *Shadows.* Forcing myself to calm down, I ask, "What did you mean when you said 'survive the shadows' like that?"

Nox glances away. His profile is magnificent, his expression defiant. "I gave you my vow that I wouldn't hunt him. I wouldn't kill him. But while the gods may be merciful, I am not. I did what Duke Haures has done to protect his human mate. I brought your ex-male to the edge of Sombra's shadows. He's no threat to you there."

My mouth falls open. He did that for me? And he thought my tears were for Connor's fate?

I swallow roughly. "I... I thought you wouldn't be able to come back."

His brow furrows. "Why?"

"Because he saw you."

"Yes." Nox turns his head so that he's looking down at me again. "But he's in Sombra now. If he finds anyone to tell about Nox the hunter, they will have heard of me." A slight, proud smile curves his lips. "I'm very well known in Nuit. He won't be giving any of my secrets away. The duke can't punish me for that."

I… I don't know what to say. Demon logic, I guess. Doesn't matter. He's here, Connor isn't, and I finally allow myself to fall apart in his arms.

He rubs his hand up and down my back. "He scared you again. I had to do something, my Amy."

"You did. You saved me," I whisper.

This is just like the night in the alley. Only, this time, I know that it's over. It's done. Connor can't come back, and my brilliant, brilliant mate found a way to get rid of him without breaking his word.

He's right. He didn't hunt him. He didn't kill him. Connor *might* survive the edge of the shadows of Sombra… but Nox told me all about his old hunting grounds.

If my ex does survive, it won't be long before he wishes he hadn't. Even then, it probably won't last.

That bloodthirsty thought shouldn't make me smile.

It does anyway.

Nox is here. Connor isn't. The duke won't be sending soldiers after us… for now, at least. And I have a roast in the oven that's probably burning at this rate.

"Come on, baby." Before anyone else sees him. I'm okay with Connor taking a one-way trip to Sombra. I'd rather he be the only one. "Let's get these groceries upstairs."

He presses a kiss to the top of my head. "Lead the way, my mate, so I can follow."

Tears still stinging my cheeks, I have to laugh.

That's my shadow demon.

Mine.

EPILOGUE

AMY

"Well," rumbles Nox as I close the front door and turn the lock. "What do you think?"

That's a pretty loaded question from my mate. And one I take a second to mull over before I answer.

What *do* I think?

Stepping over to the front window, I pull the black-out curtain to the side. It's growing dark, but even if it wasn't, we had every window treated years ago to block the bright sunlight. Nox prefers it, and since he's sacrificed so much to stay with me in the human world, the least I could do was make our home comfortable for him. That meant darkening the windows and raising the ceilings so that he could walk at his full height, and if our furniture is a casualty of his claws, that's fine. He's my mate, and if I had to return to living in the shadows of a dank, smelly alleyway to be with him, I would in a heartbeat.

Luckily, I don't have to. With Aunt Su prepared to spend the rest of her long life in Marvo with her duke, Nox and I have decided to stay in the human world for as long as we possibly could. I've never admitted it out loud, but we both know that that means until my mother—the last of my immediate family on this plane—has passed. Once nothing else is tying us here, my fierce hunter wants to start a family together in his realm.

Me, too. I'm looking forward to it, even if I'm not in any rush.

Besides, my mom is doing great. In her mid-sixties with the energy of a woman half her age, I figure we have a good twenty, thirty years before we'll relocate from my world to Nox's.

But after meeting with Shannon and Malphas just now…

What do I think? I think, now that I have proof that we're not the only mixed human-demon couple on Earth, things might be a little different… and not just because Shannon admitted that Duke Haures has already sent Glaine—freaking *Glaine*—to threaten her demon with a set of golden chains of his own.

"She thought I was twenty-six," I tell Nox at last, moving away from the window, leaning into his side. Without a moment's hesitation, he loops his arm around me, tucking me even closer. "Her eyes nearly bugged out of her head when I admitted I was forty-one."

Nox uses his other hand to swipe the edge of his shadowy claw along the height of my cheek. "Because you are a vision of beauty, my reason. That's why."

I don't know what warms me up more: the casual yet heated touch, or how he still insists after fifteen years of mating that I'm his sole reason to exist.

Or maybe it's how he's so sure that it's my appearance in general that caught Shannon off guard instead of, you know, the fact that I told her I mated my demon fifteen years ago—and I look younger than she does. No wonder she seemed to think that Nox bonded me to him against my will. It's bad enough that we really did meet when I was a kid—even if he didn't tap into our mate bond until I was in my twenties—but for her to think I was sleeping with him in my early teens… yeah. I had to nip that in the bud real quick.

My mate doesn't understand, though. Once I was a mature female, age stopped meaning a thing to him. As soon as I had his essence and our bond, I was like a Sombra demoness. I would stay at my peak maturity for the rest of time so long as Nox is alive. And since Sombra demons can only be killed by execution—and I'm pretty sure Aunt Su would have something to say about her mate offing mine—that's basically forever.

Humans don't get forever. That's a reality I have

to deal with, but I guess I didn't think it would have to be *today*.

I lay my palm over the back of his hand, purposely keeping the connection. "Thank you, baby. And I know you mean that, but she's right. I haven't aged a day since we bonded. Someone's going to notice eventually."

My mom has. Now, she doesn't say anything—she has too much tact for that—but whenever I fly down to South Carolina to visit her in her retirement, I see the way she's eyeing me closely. Add that to how she stopped asking me about my apparent lack of a love life shortly after me and Nox traded Jersey City for Connecticut ages ago, and she has to know something's up.

Probably the same way she always suspected that there was more to her sister's disappearance than she ever discovered.

We can't tell her. It's the only thing I wish was different about our happily ever after. If I could, I'd make sure my mom knew that Aunt Su is deliriously happy with her duke, that I'm absolutely loved by my mate, and she doesn't ever have to worry about either of us. But we can't. My aunt made her choice when she chose Haures, and I had to accept that to have Nox meant that he'd forever be a secret to my human life.

Except, it seems, for Shannon Crewes.

Shannon is a fellow human woman who stumbled

upon the *Grimoire du Sombra*, read the true love spell, and discovered that she was the fated mate to a Sombra demon. Not only that, but she saw my aunt's name and mine written in the book and wondered if we could help her. She searched us up on the internet, messaging me through my old Myspace account that was still online, and because I still have the same email address all these years later, I actually received it.

I'd accepted that no one in the human world would ever know about Nox or what it was like to be a demon's bonded mate. But when Shannon point-blank asked me in her message if I knew anything about Sombra, I couldn't delete the email and pretend I never saw it. I had to answer it, and Nox agreed with me. More because he wanted to make sure that, if there really was another Sombra male in the human world, he wasn't a threat to me… but he encouraged me to invite Shannon and her mate to our home.

Because that's *my* mate. The only thing that has ever mattered to him was my safety. He was willing to whisk Shannon and her unknown mate to the edge of Sombra's shadows like he had with Connor if they gave him reason to, but once I saw the way Nox clapped Malphas on the shoulder after they arrived earlier this afternoon, I knew everything would be all right.

Just in case, I turn his question around on him.

"What about you? What do you think about Shannon and Malphas?"

Nox knows what I'm doing. Even if our bond didn't make it so that we were tapped into each other constantly, he knows me better than anyone else ever has. I don't want to think about what it means that my time in the mortal world is almost over. True, I run my business from the house, but though he can't leave in case someone sees him in his demon form, I have to. For errands, for groceries, to get the mail… I can claim make-up and surgery all I want, but the world around me is visibly aging and I'm not. I'll have to confront that eventually.

Just… not now.

Bowing over me, he nuzzles the top of my hair with his chin, then pulls away. Still holding my hand, he turns me so that we're facing each other. Tilting my head back, I lose myself in his blazing red gaze.

He knows what I'm doing, but he lets me get away with it. "I knew him. Malphas. He was a clansman of mine."

I figured. There was a jolt of recognition mingled with something I couldn't quite place when Nox surged forward to greet the other demon.

"He seemed a little… nervous around you," I admit. "I wasn't sure if he was one of the good guys or not."

"He wasn't a soldier," Nox confirms. He knows exactly where my thoughts have gone. "He was the clan's artist. And you're right when you sensed his unease, my mate. As a hunter, I could be rather… harsh with some of the other males in the clan. But he's my brother, and I'm glad he found his forever in a human of his own. Malphas waited almost as long as I had for his fair-haired female." He pauses. "If she'll have him."

I don't know what they talked about, Nox and Malphas. I brought Shannon into the den with me, leaving the two males alone in the living room so they could have some privacy. I know Nox thinks that I was giving it to Shannon, but I barely know her. We'd exchanged emails and a couple of phone calls after I invited her to Madison, and I have hope that we might be friends now because of what we have in common, but Malphas was the first of his kind that Nox has seen since we left Sombra. I wanted him to have the space to process that for himself while I handled any questions my fellow human might have about mating a Sombra demon.

But if Nox and Malphas's conversation went anywhere along the same lines as the one I had with Shannon—and his comment leads me to think it did—then I know exactly what he means.

They're not mated yet. I got the impression that Shannon thought the relationship they do have is moving too quickly, especially since she told me they were already "close" a week after she summoned him into our world, but she actually is thinking about rejecting Malphas and sending him back to Sombra alone.

I guess Malphas knows that, too, otherwise Nox wouldn't have said what he did.

"She'll have to make her decision soon," he adds. "They already shared their essence. The gold moon is rising in a few days. It will be Malphas in chains if their bond isn't resolved, one way or another."

It doesn't matter that Nox lives in my world. He knows instinctively the phases of the gold moon in Sombra. Good thing, too. Sombra's second moon doesn't just act as a deadline for a mating. For the more demonic of his kind, they could lose control when it's at its peak—and any fully bonded pairs that have sex while it's high are almost guaranteed to get pregnant no matter what plane they're on.

It sucks, having to go without sex during the night of the gold moon, but unless I want to deal with having a half-human, half-demon baby in a world that's not allowed to know Nox's people exist, the most we can do is cuddle when the gold moon is out. Good thing my big mate is a phenomenal cuddler, and it'll be easy to begin our family when we're finally ready.

Just not yet. Call me selfish. Call me greedy. For now, at least, I want to spend every moment with Nox that I can without any other distractions.

Like this one.

I move into him, wrapping my arms around his

lean waist. We've learned that, when I'm touching him, he can control his shape better; as if I need an excuse to lay my hands on him. He's currently in his red-skinned demon form, heat soothing me as he holds me close.

The last fifteen years seem to have flown by in a flash. To me, it doesn't seem like there's ever been a moment I didn't have Nox in my life. As a protector, a lover, a friend… he's my mate, and I never doubted that. If it wasn't for his insistence we wait until we were in a bed, I would've bonded myself to him the very night he returned for me.

There was no *if*. Only *when*. Nox and I… we were inevitable. Fate paired us, magic united us, and he's mine as much as I'm his.

Shannon doesn't understand. Poor girl… during our talk, I got the idea that she actually believes that she might be able to walk away from her demon. If she decided to, I know without a doubt that Malphas would let her go. Sombra demons are wired that way. Their mate comes first, even before their own wants and needs. It's like how Nox willingly wore the cursed chains for all those years so that I could be free, or how he was prepared to put them on again before I claimed him in front of Duke Haures and Aunt Su. Malphas already considers the blonde his, even though they haven't finalized their mate bond yet. Shannon, though? She says she's looking for a way out. In my opinion, she's already in over her head.

That's why I gave her a few tips to make mating with her demon a little easier. I had asked her what was holding her back, not even a little surprised when her brow furrowed and she frowned, almost as if she wasn't so sure herself.

I nudged a little. Shannon didn't come right out and say it at first, but I've been where she is. Worse, I was a *virgin*. Confronted with the size of Nox's dick, I was worried about how we would fit. Shannon confessed that, though she's been with human guys before, Mal's size has her a little concerned, too. I'm not sure what she'll choose to do in the end, but at least I assured her that—as she referred to it—shadow dick is absolutely worth it.

Everything about being Nox's mate is worth it.

"She will," I tell him, turning my head so that my cheek is pressed to his bare chest. Taking one of my hands back, I trace the silver runes there. For fifteen years, he's worn my name as a brand on his skin, but I know it goes deeper than that. I'm etched on his heart, the same way he is on mine.

He rumbles in pleasure at my gentle touch. "What makes you so sure?"

"Because it's impossible to resist a Sombra demon."

Nox combs his claws through my hair. "You say that as if you tried."

"I didn't. Not even a little. I knew you were it for me."

"And you are forever my reason."

Forever. It hits me sometimes, like it did earlier when I was thinking about how I'm forever twenty-six. Forever with Nox… the idea used to be daunting. It isn't anymore. It's comforting instead, and whether we're in Connecticut, Nuit, or the privacy of Nox's shadows, it doesn't matter. I just want to be with my demon.

He wore chains for me for fourteen human years. We've been happily mated for one year longer than that, and I try every day to prove to Nox that I love him more with every passing moment.

I'm his reason. But Nox? Nox is my light in the darkness. My love. My life.

My *everything.*

And… that's the end of Amy and Nox's story, everybody! You might see them again—okay, you *will* see them again as a cameo—but the next book is bringing readers into Sombra for more than a visit! In *Bonded to the Beast*, Kennedy summons herself a Sombra demon, but something goes a little wrong when the male who is her fated mate is already fully demonic before he meets her. Loki seduces her, bonds her, and whisks her back to Sombra with him… all without her being able to understand a word of what he's saying because beastly demons can't share their essence the way other Sombra demons can.

That's not all, either! Keep reading/scrolling/clicking to find out more about Kennedy and Loki, as well as a sneak peek at Susanna and Haures's short story, coming soon :)

COMING SOON

BONDED TO THE BEAST

I didn't mean to steal the book—but I did... and now I'm in big, big trouble.

The moment I convinced one of my loyal customers to buy the leather-bound spell-book, I regretted it. At first I thought it was because I could've gotten more than fifty dollars for it—money that would've come in handy while I was on vacay—but while I was on the beach, all I kept thinking about was the book.

It called to me for some weird reason, and when I got Shannon's message that she had a question about it, I hoped that meant she would let me buy it back. Nope. She wanted to know where I got it from.

Too bad I had no idea. Almost as if by fate, it popped up in one of my boxes of stock, but I couldn't trace it. Believe me, I *tried*.

So when Shannon offered to drop it off so that I could get a closer look at it, I jumped at the chance. And that's how I found the "true love" spell in the middle of the book.

I don't know what made decide it was a good idea to read it out loud, or what came over me when the beastly shadow monster appeared in my bedroom and crooked his claw at me…

One thing led to another and, suddenly, I'm the bonded mate to a horned demon who doesn't speak English, who stole me away to terrifying world of shadows and skulls, and who I can't stop touching even so.

When I finally understand him, there's only one thing my ew mate wants to make sure is clear: I'm his. He has no intention of letting me go, either in Sombra or my world.

And it isn't long before I start to wonder if it would really be so bad to be forever bonded to the beast…

---

* *Bonded to the Beast* is the third book in the **Sombra Demons** series. It tells the story of Kennedy and Loki, the bookseller and her beast.

Releasing March 28, 2023!

COMING SOON

DRAWN TO THE DEMON DUKE

I spent years trying to decipher the old spell-book I found... and I was drawn to the duke in seconds.

I found the book in a library when I was sixteen. For the next twelve years, I made it my purpose to figure out what it was about. I'd always been interested in languages, and it amazed me that this wasn't any one I could research about.

Until I figured out that it wasn't just one language. It had its roots in Latin, with at least five other languages thrown in the mix, and once I saw the pattern, it was easy to translate the rest.

I already knew it was a spellbook. The title—Grimoire du Sombra—gave it away. But what I didn't know? Was that, after reading the whole book, I'd find a true love spell… and that it would work.

I took all of the precautions. Probably more than I needed to, but it didn't matter. When the portal opened in my living room, showing me a realm that shouldn't exist, the most awe-inspiring creature I'd ever seen strode into my room.

Duke Haures, the rule of Sombra—and, I discover, my fated mate.

Only… I'm human. His first law prevents humans from having any contact with demonkind in his realm. So what is he to do?

If your answer is to use magic to bring me back to Sombra with him, you're exactly right… and, before long, I'm more than happy to stay.

---

* *Drawn to the Demon Duke* is a prequel to the **Sombra Demons** series. It tells the story of Susanna, Amy's aunt, and how she became Duke Haures's best-kept secret.

Coming soon! Make sure to join my newsletter to learn more about this special prequel I'll be releasing exclusively there before it's available for purchase :)

AVAILABLE NOW

THE FERAL'S CAPTIVE

There's no escaping him...

Fate sucks.

As a shifter, I've always known that Fate—in the form of our goddess, the revered Luna—would have the final say when it came to my life. That includes everything: my pack, my rank, even my forever mate.

And I hate it.

I want to choose. I want my life to be mine, and if that makes me the odd one out in our pack? Oh, well. A delta, it's not like the higher ranks—our Alpha, his Beta, and the pack council—have much use for me anyway.

Still, even I'll admit I've always been drawn to the Beta of the Sylvan Pack. When I discover that he's my fated mate, it seems like giving in to the Luna's demands might not be such a bad thing after all—until he rejects me for a female he can't even have.

Because, yeah. Not only does Fate suck, it has a twisted sense of humor when it comes to me.

So that's that. I have to pretend like my broken bond isn't a constant ache while watching as my fated mate begs for table scraps from another wolf.

Is it any wonder that I start spending my free time in the woods surrounding our territory?

I wasn't afraid. Even at my low rank, I know I'm scarier than anything else that lurks in the darkness of the trees. But I was wrong—and when I see those insane golden eyes staring at me, I know I'm in deep, deep trouble.

My name is Quinn Malone, and I've just been captured by a feral…

---

* ***The Feral's Captive*** is the first in a new rejected mates paranormal romance. Set in the same world as *Never His Mate*, shifters are an open secret, most humans are off-limits, and a feral wolf shifter male is wiling to sacrifice everything to steal the wolf he believes is his mate. And though it may not be fated, Quinn and Chase's bond is just as undeniable…

AVAILABLE NOW

Keep reading for a sneak peek at the first two chapters of this book!

ONE: FATE

Fate sucks.

Rearing back my foot, I kick the baseball-sized rock in front of me. The toe of my worn leather boot connects with it, shooting it sky-high. The rock flies a good thirty feet before it pelts the thick trunk of a hickory tree in the distance. I hear the thud, my inner wolf yipping at me when the bark splits and the ancient hickory groans.

I wince. Fate still sucks, but the tree didn't deserve that.

I know better than to treat the forest with disrespect. A member of the Sylvan Pack since birth, I've lived along the edge of these woods for the last twenty-six years. They're almost as responsible for me as our Alpha is.

Probably more since I'm nothing but a delta.

We have at least fifty-six packmates at last count—

fifty-eight if Kara had her twins—and there's definitely a hierarchy. Alpha is at the top. Beta is next. Our Omega doesn't have the dominance that the higher-ranked wolves do, but her role as peacemaker for the pack is essential so she's up there; of course, being the younger sister to our Alpha doesn't hurt, either. Gammas are the older wolves who have earned a peaceful retirement after protecting the pack. Then there are deltas. Regular rank-and-file packmates, deltas make up both the bulk and the base of the hierarchy.

Of course, among deltas, there's a hierarchy of our own. Some deltas are members of Bishop's pack council. Others are patrollers; protectors who are responsible for keeping the borders of Hickory secure. We have deltas who are cooks. Who teach. Who sew. A couple of deltas are tasked with leaving pack land and mingling with humans, buying the supplies we need as a community.

And then there's me. Quinn Malone. I… I'm just a delta.

I used to have a job. I fulfilled a purpose for the Sylvan Pack. Jokingly referring to my duty as stylist/groomer, I was the one my packmates came to when they needed a haircut or—after one memorable tumble through the blackberry bushes with his mate—they had canes and tangled thorns all up in their fur. I'd needed my clippers that day, and Frankie's wolf had a bald ass for a week after that.

But that was before.

Something similar happened to Sophia. I should've anticipated my fate after seeing hers, but I hadn't. That was my fault.

Sophia is the female half of our Alpha couple. Bishop's mate, she came from the River Run Pack on the East Coast where she taught the local pups math and science. When the Luna whispered her name to Bishop during his Alpha ceremony five years ago, he sent for her, and she accepted his mate bond. They performed the Luna Ceremony during the full moon that followed, and, once they were fully bonded, she was no longer a plain, boring, nobody delta like me.

Her dominance level didn't change by mating Bishop, but her rank sure did. From the bottom to the top, she couldn't be a math teacher anymore. Being the Alpha's forever mate was a full-time job of its own.

So is being the Beta's mate, I've discovered.

That's supposed to be me, but it isn't, and I'm still shit out of luck when it comes to my place in our pack after all this time—and all because of the Luna and her twisted idea of Fate.

Six months ago, I smiled at Weston Reed, the Beta of the Sylvan Pack. I'd done it a hundred times before. We were friends, growing up in the same age group, even though being a born beta wolf meant he was a much higher rank than us deltas. I knew that, one day, West would succeed our old Beta, Harris, and it didn't hurt to be buddy-buddy with him while he still rubbed elbows with the rest of us.

Truth be told, I'd always been drawn to him, but friendship was all he could offer so I took it gladly. For as long as I could remember, he had been together with Helene, our pack's Omega. And while their official relationship ended about three years back when Helene was promised to the future Alpha of a neighboring pack, West… he didn't get the memo.

He's been trying to convince her to choose him over Rafael ever since. Still is even now.

I was on his side when the pronouncement first came. As much as I had a crush on West, he loved Helene. I knew that. Anyone with eyes could see that. I thought she loved him, too. She didn't have to leave Hickory when Rafael eventually became Alpha if she didn't want to. She could reject him and choose West instead.

She refused. Pack gossip said that she was content to wait until Rafael could claim her by shifter tradition. That she had decided to accept her fated mate. It also said that Helene gently suggested that West do the same.

But *he* refused to do that—and, six months ago, when I smiled at him and, suddenly, something snapped into place, our goddess whispering to me that West was *mine*… he still refused the idea of taking any mate other than Helene.

Worse, he *rejected* me.

He rejected the idea that *I* could ever be the female meant for him.

Oh, not with words, though. That's not West's style. He's never been cruel. He just pretended that he didn't feel it when a bond sprang up between us, and because he's the Beta, the rest of the pack did the same.

One problem: ignoring the bond doesn't mean it isn't there.

Following his lead, I stayed away, too. I didn't push him. I gave him the space he needed to work out his feelings for Helene before he did what nearly every other shifter did and claimed his fated mate as his own.

But Fate sucks, remember? And West is the rare wolf who seems to be able to fight her pull.

I just wish *I* could.

Even worse, the pack still considers me his mate. Does it matter that West doesn't? Nope. The Luna says I'm the Beta's mate, so I am.

You know what that means?

No one comes to me for a haircut anymore. They don't want to bother the Beta's mate for something so trivial, and now Gregory is the new pack stylist.

I've gone from a flirtatious she-wolf needing to fight off interested males to basically being the shifter version of a freaking nun, only without a wimple. None of the males treat me like a prospective mate anymore. Why would they when they already believe I'm taken?

Worst of all is how when other packmates need West, they come to me as if I hold any sway over him. Then they apologize when I point out that they'd have better luck going to Helene.

I was understanding in the beginning. As much as I was over the moon to discover I was meant for West, I knew he loved Helene. I just thought… maybe he could love me, too.

But, once again, I was wrong.

Ugh!

I don't kick another rock, but that's only because I still feel guilty for striking the tree before. This is my safe place. The clearing on the edge of pack territory where I can go to bitch and rage and get out all of my frustrations before I go back to Hickory where all I have to look forward to are pitying looks.

They all know I'm the rejected mate. The one cast aside. West never had to say it, but it's obvious.

And that makes it so much harder to take.

One of the downsides to being the Beta's forgotten mate? If I'm gone too long, West won't even notice—but someone else in the pack will.

I lose track of how long I was sitting on the grass, absently weaving flowers into my hair. I used to keep it short, usually shoulder-length, but in the last six months, I let it grow. I guess I lost the taste for cutting even my own hair, and now the deep black strands go nearly past my boobs when I'm standing up.

Hiding out in this clearing isn't new to me. I've been coming here since I was a randy teen and I needed a place to meet up with shifter males who wanted nothing more than a good time. I've never been the type of virginal, holier-than-thou she-wolf who wanted to wait until I took a mate. Shifters are earthy creatures. Sex is a biological urge. And, fuck it, it just feels amazing when done right.

I haven't been laid in six months. That's my longest dry spell since I started crooking my finger at horny males, inviting them to join me out beneath the hickories. Maybe that's why I'm feeling kind of twitchy all of a sudden.

My skin feels like it's stretched over my bones. Letting go of the wildflower I plucked, I rub my neck. A bird sings in the distance. My shifter's ears tune in. I hear… I hear…

Rustling?

The twitchy feeling turns into something else. Unless I'm imagining it, it's like I feel eyes on me. Like someone's watching me.

But who? There aren't many who come this far. Most of my packmates prefer to stay close to the cluster of cabins where we each have our homes. The pack circle is there—the cleared area with picnic tables where we can meet and talk and eat together—and it's within reach of the Alpha cabin where Bishop lives with Sophia.

I've brought plenty of males here over the years, but none recently. And those who know that I consider this part of the woods mine would never approach without permission. This is my territory, and a male encroaching on a possessive she-wolf learns very quickly how far she'll go to protect what's hers.

Especially because I never would've found it if it wasn't for West.

Before he was the Beta, he was another shifter who enjoyed exploring the woods. He showed me this spot years ago and I immediately proclaimed it as mine. He didn't mind; he already had his own. While I came out here for the peace and, later, the privacy, West always visited a grove on the far borders of Hickory where countless types of wildflowers grew; similar to the ones that are growing by me, but more plentiful. It was a thing he had with Helene. Whenever they were separated during the time they were a couple, he'd bring a flower back for her.

They're not a couple anymore, but he still does it. I used to think it was cute. These days, though, I get a funny feeling deep in the pit of my stomach whenever I see him from a distance, stalking toward the Omega cabin, a stem clutched between his fingers.

I did a few weeks ago. Just like now, I'd sensed

someone near a few seconds before my wolf started to whine once she recognized West's. He was in the woods, and he found me on my own, even stopping to say hello for the first time in ages… but all I could focus on was the flower in his hand.

Is that who is out there now? Should I go look?

Will my battered heart handle it when I see him holding another flower for Helene?

This isn't the first time I've longed to get up and run to West. Once again I'm sitting here, wondering if I should work up the nerve to head upwind and confront him in his own private sanctuary out in the woods.

It's getting harder to resist. I have to remind myself that he's chosen Helene, and I'm better off by myself—even if I'm not.

So, yeah. That's my big secret. My dark shame. I pretend like it doesn't faze me one bit that my fated mate follows another female around like a besotted puppy dog. On the rare occasion one of my old friends tries to see how I'm doing, I shrug and say that it happens. If the Luna got it right every time, there would be no rejected mates. No broken bonds.

Heck, one of the biggest cautionary tales in the shifter world is Jack "Wicked Wolf" Walker, a cruel Alpha who—at one time—ruled almost the entire West Coast of shifters. He turned his pack into a haven known as the Wolf District, and he ruled it with an ever-changing retinue of Betas—and no mate. His fated mate rejected him before he bonded her to him, choosing to mate the Alpha of a nearby pack instead.

It's an open secret. While the Wicked Wolf was still alive, everyone knew why he went through she-wolves the way I used to go through males. After losing his fated mate, he didn't want to choose another. He was happy by himself, and he was one of the most powerful—and feared—Alphas in the United States until a challenger finally caught up to him.

I heard it was a vamp. Makes sense. Those blood-suckers can be *brutal.*

I try to tell myself that I could be like the Wicked Wolf. Not the sadistic bastard part, but a shifter who didn't let the pain of a jagged bond stop him from living life to the fullest.

Unlike me.

Another rustle and, unless I'm imagining it, I swear I hear a snuffling sound.

I take a deep breath, trying to see if I catch a familiar scent. I'm out here so often that I can recognize the wild wolves that visit, the prey animals that skirt around our territory, even the other shifters who take a break from pack living by passing through.

Is there a whiff of sandalwood?

I exhale. Nope.

Nothing. I get nothing. Everything is the same as usual.

And that makes the weight of the stare on me even weirder…

Brushing my hands against my jeans, I rise up from the ground. The sensation that someone is close by is only growing stronger. I can't shake the feeling that I'm being watched.

Maybe it's a packmate. Maybe it is West. Maybe it's someone—or some*thing*—else entirely.

Whatever it is, I don't like it.

I'm not scared, though. Please. I'm a wolf shifter. There's nothing out there I can't take.

Well, maybe not a vampire, but you have to be much more dominant than me to take on a vampire. Good thing you can scent one of those undead corpses from a mile away. Between their icy auras and the scent of blood and rotten meat that clings to their supernaturally beautiful forms, they'd never get close enough to Hickory before the whole pack would work together to take them down.

Still, scared or not, I've been out here too long. The last thing I need is Bishop sending West after me again. It's always super awkward when I have to talk to him. We have an unspoken agreement to pretend we're strangers most of the time, and whenever we don't, it's fucking terrible.

Just like it was a couple of weeks ago when I hated the azalea he held almost as much as I wish I could hate my fated mate…

I want him. He doesn't want me.

Fate sucks, and there's not a damn thing I can do about it.

So, just in case, I might as well go home.

Purposely giving my back to whoever—*whatever*—might be out there watching me, I start to jog back toward Hickory. It isn't long before I leave that strange sensation behind me. By the time I cross back into the inner border of pack land, I've forgotten all about it.

I want to go straight to my cabin. I'm not in the mood to deal with any of my packmates today. I'd had a decent enough afternoon in the woods. Maybe I'll feel like being social tomorrow.

Of course, then I hear someone call my name from off to my side.

"Quinn!"

The voice is familiar and, for a split second, hope fills my chest. And, sure, his aura marks him as a delta, and he doesn't smell like sandalwood like West does, but I'm so far gone over my fated mate that I'm willing to be delusional until I turn toward him and see—

"Tucker." Crap. "How have you been?"

His smile is blinding. Something about Tucker Madden always reminds me of toothpaste commercials I see on television. He has bright white teeth, gleaming golden eyes, and dark blond hair styled in soft waves. Like all protectors, he has a lean body that I know intimately.

From the heat in his eyes as he looks me up and down, he's thinking the same thing about me.

"Missing you, but other than that I'm alright. I've been thinking about how much fun we used to have. Good times, huh?"

"Yeah. Sure."

"I was also thinking… it's been a while. You know. You and me. Maybe we could have some fun again? Go visit that spot in the woods you like? I know it's not too far. And it's real nice and private."

Ah, Luna. As if I need another reminder that I'm single as fuck. With West making his rejection obvious, the males I used to fool around with still see me as a sure thing—but they're the only ones.

Funnily enough, even they left me alone for the first few months. West is our Beta, and he has the respect of the entire pack. I'm his fated mate, and they figured he'd come to his senses eventually and accept that.

But he didn't. In so many different ways, he continues to reject me. To reject our bond. Tucker coming up and reminding me about old times isn't an insult to West so long as the Beta acts like I'm nothing to him. Tucker is just a horny male shifter who wants to get his rocks off, that's all.

And he probably guesses I'm the hard-up she-wolf who might say yes to his offer because he doesn't try to be coy or sly at all when he says, "I'm going on patrol after dinner, but that gives me a good hour. I was heading out to take a walk in the woods now anyway. You want to join me?"

A walk in the woods… every adventurous shifter in Hickory knows what that's a euphemism for.

I should. The longer I stew over a male I can't have, the more bitter I'm becoming. Maybe a quick romp with another packmate is just what I need to get my mind off of West.

But I can't. As insane as it sounds to want to be loyal to a male who doesn't want you, if I sneak off with Tucker, it's almost like I'm cheating on my fated mate.

Speaking of—

My wolf yips when she senses him. The little hairs on my human arm stand up, almost like I've been shocked by a tiny jolt of electricity. I instinctively know where he is and, shifting my stance a few degrees to the right, I look over Tucker's lean shoulder.

And there he is.

Weston Reed, the Beta of the Sylvan Pack.

My heart stutters in my chest. I'd always thought he was good-looking before. Since the bond appeared, he's more than that.

He's *breathtaking* to me.

West isn't as conventionally handsome a male as Tucker is. He wears his dark brown hair cut short, and his eyes are unusual for a shifter. Normally dark grey, they only turn gold when he's lost control of his emotions. Since that's almost never for a disciplined beta wolf like West, I've only ever seen it happen twice: the day we recognized each other as fated mates, and when he discovered that Helene was fated to belong to Rafael Cruces once he took over his pack.

West isn't alone. Though it takes a second for me to stop staring at his profile, I force myself to look away from him. Even before my gaze lands on the beautiful, blonde Helene Dupuis, I knew exactly who he was talking to.

The look of pure adoration on his masculine features made it obvious.

My heart aches. There's no other way to describe it. My fated mate is right there, barely twenty feet away, and I've never felt farther apart from him.

And wouldn't you know, I'm also not alone.

My heart still aches while my stomach sinks.

I shake my head. "Maybe some other time, Tucker."

Tucker follows the direction of my stare, making a soft sound of understanding when he sees West and Helene together.

"Yeah. Well, you know where to find me." He reaches his hand out to pat me on the shoulder. I try not to wince when he pauses, only an inch separating us, careful not to actually make contact. "Until next time, Quinn."

He couldn't touch me. West is over there making

goo-goo eyes at Helene, Tucker wanted in my pants two minutes ago, and once he noticed the Beta nearby, he couldn't even touch me.

Until next time?

Yeah. I don't think there's going to be one.

TWO: POISON

Sometimes I wish that West would just reject me completely.

It's easy enough. Up until the moment we perform the Luna Ceremony and get her blessing, all it takes is one half of a promised pair saying the words with meaning: "I reject you." *Boom.* The bond snaps, and though I'll have lost any chance of ever having my fated mate, at least I wouldn't be existing in this state of constant ache.

I know he doesn't mean to give me hope. He never has. In his own way, the Beta is being a decent wolf. He knows how much it'll hurt me to hear the truth so he just doesn't say it.

He doesn't have to.

As Beta, he's the second highest-ranked wolf in our pack. Bishop is first, and though we have two other budding alphas living in Hickory, West ranks higher than them because of his title. He's Bishop's right-hand wolf, the only one—besides Sophia—who can look Bishop in the eye without immediately baring his throat in submission. All of our fellow packmates follow his lead. As soon as he pointedly ignored the fact that the Luna paired us up, so did everyone else.

As far as the Sylvan Pack is concerned, West rejected me in every way that mattered—except actually setting me free.

I must be a fucking glutton for punishment. I walk around like a pariah, the topic of whispers and rumors that they know me and my wolf can hear. They feel pity for me, but they also wonder why I don't just leave.

Sometimes I wonder the same exact thing.

Hickory is my home. I was born on this land, and until the Luna upended my life, I planned on dying on it. My dad did—a victim of a challenge against another delta that he didn't win—and my mom, unable to live without her lifemate, who followed soon after.

I was twelve when all that happened. The rest of the Sylvan Pack rallied around me, giving me time to mourn, but also making sure I didn't want for anything. If I walk away because I can't have the one male meant for me, it's like I failed or something. I've never given up when things got hard. I'm stubborn to a fault.

Petty, too, I admit. If I have to live with the urge to go to West every single day, I'm not gonna make it easy for him to get out of doing the same. He's gonna see me. I know what an unfulfilled bond feels like. No matter how much he loves Helene, it's hard to beat Fate.

Am I hoping that he might wake up one day and realize what he's been missing out on? Not really. Maybe at first I did. If so, it was short-lived.

Am I waiting for Helene to leave Hickory for her promised mate?

I… I might be.

I'm not sure what that says about me. I never wanted to be another she-wolf's sloppy seconds or a male's second choice. During my wild early years, when I was exploring my sexuality without the pesky complications of settling down with a mate, I had half the males in my age group sniffing around my tail. All I had to do was run into the woods, content in the knowledge that an interested male would chase.

Not West. Never West. He's always been hovering over Helene.

No one knows when she'll be leaving the pack. As our Omega—and the Alpha's beloved younger sister—Helene will stay in Hickory until her promised mate performs the Alpha Ceremony, taking over the Gravetail Pack. Only then will they perform the Luna Ceremony that will bond them together, and West will finally have to accept that he can't have the mate he wants.

Will he come crawling back to me?

I don't know.

Will I be waiting for him if he does?

I… I don't know that, either.

Another reason why I wish I could just get rid of this pull I feel for him. After the last six months of pity and need and loneliness, there's a good chance I would jump him the first time he acted like he wanted to be with me.

A she-wolf's gotta have some pride, right? When it comes to West Reed, I'm pretty sure I don't.

Ugh.

He won't do it. He won't snap our bond. Why? I have no clue. But six months after we both recognized that we were fated, all he's done is grow colder, more distant, while focusing all of his intention on a female he can never have.

And me? I spend all of my time on the edge of Hickory. Still near enough to the pack that I don't accidentally become a lone wolf, but with enough space that I can shake off the mantle of being the Beta's rejected mate.

There are other options. If Helene *did* forsake her own fated mate and choose West, our bond would break. Even less likely, I could choose another male. Since my packmates would never dare try to steal their Beta's mate—though, as Tucker proved the other day, fucking me is okay, but mating me is definitely a no-no—and I have no intention of leaving Hickory, I'm gonna have to just suck it up and get used to being the pack outcast.

It's like I've got a scarlet letter on my damn chest. Only, instead of Hester Prynne's A, I've got an R.

R for rejected. Yippee!

You know, I've heard rumors about a Luna-touched female with the gift—or curse, depending on your point of view—of breaking bonds with her little finger. One touch and, so long as one of the mates was willing, it was as though it never existed.

As much as it must suck to be her, if she's real, maybe I should see if I could track her down. With West content to go on as if our bond doesn't exist, she might be the best chance I have.

I'm just thinking about which of my packmates might know more about the mysterious Luna-touched female when, suddenly, a very familiar aura wraps around me. Just like the other day when I was talking to Tucker, I sense him before I pick up his scent, and by the time I turn to find West walking toward me, all I can think is: Mate. *Mate. Maaaaate.*

As handsome as ever, his face is an expressionless mask. I can't tell if his thoughts are running along the same lines as mine or if he was even expecting to run into me like this in the first place.

I peer closer. There's a look in his eye I recognize. Shortly after Bishop proclaimed him as his

Beta—and long before I realized he was my fated mate—I used to tease him that it was his "business" look.

Wonderful.

"Quinn. There you are."

As if he's surprised to find me. Whether he wants to admit it or not, with our bond open, he's as viscerally aware of me as I am of him. It wouldn't have taken much to know that I was sitting on the front porch of my cabin.

Unless… unless he keeps our bond closed on his side. It takes a lot of effort to cut off a mate, and it would probably be more uncomfortable than leaving it unfulfilled, but it *is* possible. I don't do it because, really, what's the point?

Is that what he's doing to me?

I don't ask. I can't. Honestly, I'd rather not know the answer.

Instead, I shrug. "Yup. What's going on? You need me for something?"

Please need me…

He nods. "I know you spend a lot of time out among the hickories and the oaks on the edge of our territory." Gee… I wonder why. "Some of our patrols have picked up a few unfamiliar tracks recently. No scent, and that's what's weird about them. You should probably stick closer to the heart of pack land until we figure out what's going on."

My heart stutters against my ribcage. I don't want

to read too much into West coming to warn me personally, but…

"Are you telling this me because you're the Beta and I'm a packmate, or because—"

West's perfectly chiseled jaw goes tight. "Because I'm the Beta and I have a duty to every wolf in Hickory."

Right. Message received.

So we both know where we stand. As if I wasn't already aware.

I offer him a mock salute. "Will do. Thanks."

West nods. His dark grey eyes travel over the fake smile I pulled on my face. For a second, I think he wants to say something else. I'm almost begging him to.

He doesn't.

With another nod and a short wave, he turns on his heel and starts to walk away. Probably going to see Helene again.

I wait a moment. When he doesn't turn to glance over his shoulder at me, I think about West's warning—and then I completely blow it off.

I'm not worried about there being a threat in the woods. True, I could've sworn I felt someone watching me the other day, but nothing happened. If it was really that big of an issue, Bishop would forbid any of us from heading out there instead of just giving us a warning. He'd amp up pack patrols on the edge of our territory, too.

Besides, I'm scarier than anything else that could be out there. I'll be fine.

And if this is my own way of saying, "Fuck you," to West without it being a challenge, then that makes my decision to retreat to the woods again that much sweeter.

The best thing about being a delta? I'm not important enough that I can't slip away without one of the higher-ranked packmates noticing.

If I'm gone too long, they will. Our pack is strongest when we're whole. Bishop takes his role as Alpha seriously. If he can't account for all of us at any given moment, it sets off his wolf—and that usually sets off West.

It's bad enough I ran into West a couple of weeks ago, carrying another Luna-damned flower for his precious Helene. No doubt in my mind that it was an accident, and that he only stopped to talk to me because his wolf spurred him to. With all of Hickory between us, he can usually avoid me. When we're that close? Even he isn't strong enough to resist the pull. Part of the reason I call bullshit on his warning me about the woods earlier today. Sure, he's the Beta, but any other protector could've done the same thing. It didn't have to be West.

Of course, then I remember how, after I ran into

Tucker a few days back, I saw West watching Helene with such open adoration—the Omega the only one worthy of him showing any hint of emotion toward—and I realize I'm still fooling myself.

Come on, Quinn. He's just one male. One dick. If he can beat Fate, so can I.

Right?

Well, not in the last six months I haven't…

Our tie has another downside besides the fact that it rules me: if I'm missing for too long, Bishop will definitely send West in particular to find me. Neither of us wants that. He'd be able to, too, and not only because he's the Beta. Mates can find each other by following their bond to the other end; unless it's closed off, of course. It's how I know that, whenever he's not busy with his pack duties, West spends all of his free time outside of Helene's cabin, waiting for her to give him a moment of her attention.

Me? I spend mine in the woods.

That afternoon, as I move soundlessly through the trees, I rub my chest with the heel of my hand.

It's getting worse. Can't deny it anymore. The jagged edge of our neglected mate bond… it *hurts*. At this point, if I could use my claws to gut myself open and rip it out, I would. Anything has to be better than walking around with the sting of rejection as my constant companion.

Usually just being close enough to take in West's

scent soothes it for a little while. Talking to him, hearing his voice… it helps.

Not today, though.

When I get to the small clearing I consider mine, I plop down on the ground. My legs are stretched out in front of me, I'm leaning back on my hands, my eyes cast toward the sky. The caps of leaves on the crowded hickory trees block out most of the sunlight, leaving a few stray beams filtering through.

I exhale roughly. It's not much, but at least I find some peace here.

Later, I'll look back and accept that everything that happened next wouldn't have if I'd only swallowed my pride and listened to West's warning. But I didn't, and by the time I discovered there was some merit in it, it's too late.

A big, black wolf has stalked out of the woods about twenty feet away from me.

I only noticed because his eyes are a vibrant gold, and as shadows fell around me, their shine caught my attention. I never scented him. Never heard him. I don't know where he came from or how he snuck up on me, but it doesn't matter. He's here.

Lips parted, I breathe in deep, sampling scents. Big mistake. Something burns the back of my throat.

I choke.

Wolfsbane.

No wonder I didn't catch his scent before his eyes flickered in the distance. No wonder the pack patrol found prints and no other trace. Wolfsbane can cover up anything except muddy prints.

He's not a real wolf. I hadn't thought he was, but the wolfsbane gives him away. That's a shifter out there. The wolfsbane makes it worse. He's not only a stranger, but he has to be an enemy. No supe with good intentions carries wolfsbane on them.

And that's when his aura rushes at me. It took a few seconds, thanks to the wolfsbane messing with my senses, but I can't miss it now.

He's a shifter—and he's an alpha. Explains why he's so huge.

The way his gaze is locked on me also explains why he's here.

I have no clue what the hell he wants with me, but there's no denying the predatory gleam in his gaze as he pads closer.

He's moving slowly on purpose. He doesn't want to spook me. He's treating me like prey and, Luna, does that rankle.

I hop to my feet. He pauses, then continues to stalk forward.

My first instinct is to shift. I run faster as a wolf. His every move screams he's ready to take off if I do, and I'm not sure I can waste the precious seconds it would cost me to explode out of my clothes and change shapes.

I'm still a wolf whether I'm in my skin or not. I know these woods like the back of my hand. I know every member of the Sylvan Pack. The black wolf is undeniably a stranger. So he tiptoed up to the edge of our territory. I can lose him, then make it further into Hickory where the rest of the pack can help me.

That's what we do. When push comes to shove, we help each other.

I bolt. Just like I figured, he comes racing after me.

I can make it. Weaving around the trees, taking the quickest path back toward Hickory, I can lose him—

Nope.

With all of his brute strength, the wolf barrels into my legs. It's a cheap shot. I'm lucky he didn't snap a bone with his impact, and when I go flying before landing on my belly in the dirt, all of the air is knocked out of me.

A second later, his wolfish body is covering my human one.

Shit. I knew he was big, but pressed against me, I realize he's *massive.*

What *is* he?

He looks like a wolf, but he sure doesn't act like one. Wolves rarely give pursuit when they're hunting. They prefer to ambush their prey.

Then again, isn't that what he's done to me?

Once I'm down, I figure it's worth the split second of vulnerability. The force of my shift will tear my clothes off of my back, but the supernatural magic inherent to our kind will also push him away from me if only for a second.

That might be all I need to get away from him. My wolf is much squirmier than my human form. Faster, too. Shifting now should give me the best chance of escaping him.

I'm quick. He's quicker. As if he expected me to change shapes once he got a hold of me, he grabs my scruff between his fangs. Though, as a shifter, I only have sex when I'm in my skin, never my fur, there are some primal memories I can't deny. A wolf on top of me, his fangs pinning me by the scruff?

He's mounting my wolf.

No fucking way.

He's an alpha. Not as strong as Bishop—as if anyone could be—he's still twice my size and probably triple my power. He must've thought I was an easy target.

If so, he was wrong.

I jerk my head. His fangs rip through my skin. Ignoring the pain, I whirl on him, snapping my fangs back, trying to bite any part of him I can reach. I'm especially partial to any dangly bits. An unknown wolf attacking me on pack land? I have every right to defend myself, and if he ends up castrated, he'll learn that even a low-ranking delta she-wolf has claws and fangs.

I lock onto his foreleg. Blood gushes into my mouth. Swallowing it greedily, I tear.

Feel that, asshole!

The wolf growls. Instead of trying to get me off of him, he pushes against my fangs, feeding me more of his fur, his muscle, his blood.

I choke on it. Breathing through my snout, I refuse to let go.

He shifts. I'm ripping human flesh now, but I don't care. In fact, without the fur in my way, I'm sure I'm doing more damage.

Why isn't he fighting to be free? Or fighting back? From his aura, I can tell he's an alpha. Just because I'm defending myself, it doesn't mean that he won't take this as me answering his challenge. By shifter law, he can put me down without any consequence. He's certainly strong enough to. Failing that, bastard could force me to submit. He's too dominant for me to ignore.

I'd never win.

Only… he isn't. He's willingly allowing me to gnaw on him as the heat of his naked body pushes me to the ground.

I stay in my fur. I need my fangs to be at their sharpest, I need my jaw to be strong, and I need to keep my naked human body away from the monster erection digging into my back.

That's not the only thing I feel poking me.

Still clamping down on him—now that he's human, his foreleg is now his upper arm—I jerk in time to see he has something in his other hand. I don't know where he got it from. Clothes never survive the shift so it's not like he pulled it out of a pocket. Jewelry that's been charmed might, but he's not holding a necklace or a bracelet.

That's a shot. The vial is filled with a viscous, silvery grey liquid that shimmers against the glass casing—and he's buried the needle part of the injector past my fur.

I know what that is, too.

Mercury.

Quicksilver.

Poison.

Before I can react, he uses his thumb to press down on the plunger at the top of the injector.

Fucker.

It's not enough to kill me—he'd need pure silver to do that—but quicksilver isn't just a poison. It's also a sedative. Pour a couple of drops in a drink and it'll do something funny to a shifter's beast. Shoot one with an injection of the stuff and I'm gonna be on my ass before I know it.

He runs his fingers through the fur on the top of my head, obviously pleased with himself. His mouth reaches one of my ears. I flick it angrily, but that doesn't stop him from leaning closer.

"Remember," he whispers in a gruff voice, "it didn't have to be this way."

As the quicksilver worms its way through me and I

start to go under, I suddenly remember something I should never have forgotten.

Real wolves will rarely pursue prey. But give a wolf shifter the chance?

He'll *always* chase.

I also realize something else.

There's no escaping him, either.

KEEP IN TOUCH

Stay tuned for what's coming up next! Follow me at any of these places — or sign up for my newsletter — for news, promotions, upcoming releases, and more:

>> Newsletter <<

ALSO BY SARAH SPADE

Holiday Hunk

Halloween Boo

This Christmas

Auld Lang Mine

I'm With Cupid

Getting Lucky

When Sparks Fly

Holiday Hunk: the Complete Series

Claws and Fangs

Leave Janelle

Never His Mate

Always Her Mate

Forever Mates

Hint of Her Blood

Taste of His Skin

Stay With Me

Never Say Never: Gem & Ryker

Sombra Demons

Drawn to the Demon Duke*

Mated to the Monster

Stolen by the Shadows

Santa Claws

Bonded to the Beast

Stolen Mates

The Feral's Captive

Chase and the Chains

The Beta's Bride

Wolves of Winter Creek

(part of Kindle Vella)

Prey

Pack

Predator

Claws Clause

(written as Jessica Lynch)

Mates **free*

Hungry Like a Wolf

Of Mistletoe and Mating

No Way

Season of the Witch

Rogue

Sunglasses at Night

Ain't No Angel **free*

True Angel

Ghost of Jealousy

Night Angel

Broken Wings

Of Santa and Slaying

Lost Angel

Born to Run

Uptown Girl

Ordinance 7304: the Bond Laws (Claws Clause Collection #1)

Living on a Prayer (Claws Clause Collection #2)

Lightning Source UK Ltd.
Milton Keynes UK
UKHW011256260223
417690UK00004B/138